VENGEANCE AT BITTERSWEET

Always a loner, Largo reckoned it was the reason for his survival as a bounty hunter. But things change when he has to join forces with Colonel Sebastian Kyte in the hunt for a band of desperate killers. Kyte is not interested in financial rewards. So what is the old Confederate soldier's game? And how does a Kiowa medicine man's daughter figure in the final showdown at Bittersweet? Vengeance is sweet, but it comes with a heavy price tag.

Books by Dale Graham
in the Linford Western Library:

NUGGET!

DALE GRAHAM

VENGEANCE AT BITTERSWEET

Complete and Unabridged

LINFORD
Leicester

First published in Great Britain in 2006 by
Robert Hale Limited
London

First Linford Edition
published 2007
by arrangement with
Robert Hale Limited
London

British Library CIP Data

Graham, Dale
    Vengeance at Bittersweet.—Large print ed.—
Linford western library
    1. Bounty hunters—Fiction 2. Western stories
    3. Large type books
    I. Title
    823.9'14 [F]

    ISBN 978–1–84617–700–2

Published by
F. A. Thorpe (Publishing)
Anstey, Leicestershire

Set by Words & Graphics Ltd.
Anstey, Leicestershire
Printed and bound in Great Britain by
T. J. International Ltd., Padstow, Cornwall

This book is printed on acid-free paper

1

Carlsbad Junction

Inside the railroad depot, it was hotter than a whore's bedchamber. Dust motes floating in the static air were reflected in the beams of sunlight arrowing in through the open doorway. The clerk laid down his pen and stroked the film of sweat from his frazzled brow. Within seconds it was replaced. Even with all the windows wide open, there was no escape from the sweltering heat.

Carlsbad Junction was a minor railroad halt. Goods were dropped off here for collection by local ranchers and business people in the widely scattered settlements to the north and west. All it comprised was a single depot office and storage outbuildings, plus the ubiquitous water storage tank. This part of southern New Mexico was very sparsely populated and the daily train always stopped here to take on water and logs.

'Damn blasted country!'

Henry Tasker could cuss to Hell and back, but he still had to complete the inventory recently unloaded from the noon train. For the umpteenth time that day, his beady eyes peered at the wall clock. It was Friday. Another four hours and he could head north, back home to Buckeye for the weekend. His thick lips drooled at the thought. A warm soft bed and some decent grub for a change. Not to mention a loving and responsive wife. Henry smiled luridly at the prospect.

Due in no small measure to the distance involved, he was forced to sleep over during the week relying on the various railroad conductors to supply him with victuals. He automatically flicked a buzzing fly from his bulbous snout, then lifted the pen to resume his tally of the various orders.

The white shirt, itchy and rather soiled after five days of wear, stuck to his back.

'What I wouldn't give for a tankard of ice-cold beer,' he muttered to himself scowling at the bottle of tepid ale on his desk.

To prevent it bubbling over in the heat, he kept the bottles of liquid refreshment in a bowl filled with water. He poured a liberal measure into a glass and raised it to his open mouth. It slid down his gullet like an over-ripe peach. Henry gave a contented sigh — just so long as the line manager didn't happen along. The Southern Pacific Railroad Company had strict rules about drinking on the job. Only the previous week, a colleague of Henry's, two stops down the line at Orogrande, had been sacked when the manager had paid an impromptu visit. And not by train either. He had wrong-footed Jeb Stone by coming overland from the county seat at Roswell. And that was it. Pension forfeited and no reference.

The thought that such a fate could befall a married man with two kids quickly brought Henry Tasker to his feet. This time it wasn't the unremitting heat that elicited beads of moisture on his brow. Sliding the liquid evidence into the bottom drawer of his desk, the rotund depot clerk automatically straightened his necktie and made a rapid exit of the office. His short plump legs padded along the junction's raised platform.

Piggy eyes flitted about nervously. It would be just like that nosy critter to turn up on a Friday hoping to catch him out. He made a circuit of the depot squinting his gritty peepers against the harsh glare.

All the way to the distant mountains of the Guadalupes, the endless sea of dull ochre scrubland oscillated in waves of heat. If he hadn't been privy to this sight constantly over the last two years, he could have sworn blind he was looking at a glistening lake; a rippling expanse of cool blue water beckoning to the parched traveller. But Henry knew it was just an illusion, a mirage that had driven men crazy. To the unwary, the New Mexico desert was a pitiless mistress, and spitefully disparaging to the ill-equipped.

Except for the swaying thermals, nothing moved.

Henry sighed with relief. No surprise guest, thankfully.

He was just turning with the more confident intention of finishing the bottle, when a slight movement impinged itself on his eye line. Hooded eyes narrowed as he focused on the far horizon. At first nothing.

Then he saw it.

A rider, the dark profile of his upper body floating on the heat waves.

Could it be the line manager?

Henry's jaw dropped. Screwing his eyes tighter, he could just pick out the wide-brimmed Stetson, then the grey jogging head of a cayuse. That wasn't his boss. Too big and wide. Henry relaxed. Realizing he had been holding his breath, a long hiss of constricted air whistled from between taut lips. Then he went back into the office to finish off the bottle.

★   ★   ★

Beneath the turned-down brim of the battered brown hat, hawkish grey eyes like sharp chips of flint crinkled around the edges. The rider's steady gaze was fixed purposefully on the distant rail depot. At least five days' dark stubble streaked with dust concealed a face chiselled from pure granite. Lips, thin and dry, drew back in a tight smile.

Largo was more than pleased that he had managed to navigate an accurate course across the Brazos country of West Texas into the territory of New Mexico to his objective. And there it was, dead ahead — the rail depot at Carlsbad Junction. Holding the grey mare to a gentle trot, the rider sat easy in the saddle. Large gnarled hands rested on the pommel, never far from the carved ivory grip of a well-oiled Colt Frontier revolver that was clearly not there for display purposes.

Save for the rhythmic creak of saddle leather, all was silent.

As far back as his memory could recall, he had been referred to only as Largo. At one time, there must have been some other name. But the hard-nosed rannie had grown up as a tough street kid who knew no other. Early on in life, he had learned to fend for himself. It had been a matter of survival.

Abandoned at an early age on the front steps of St Xavier's Catholic Mission in the Texas border town of Presidio, he had been raised by the resident priest. Father Augustus had reluctantly accepted the waif into his fold. There the boy had joined a heap of similar flotsam that nobody wanted.

The good father had been a strict and brutal disciplinarian. At times Largo sensed that he positively enjoyed lording it over his dependent flock. After feeling the sharp end of the priest's leather belt once too often, young Largo had taken it upon himself to administer his own brand of justice.

It was six weeks before Father Augustus was able to sit down without wincing. In the meantime, Largo had felt it advisable to seek his fortune elsewhere. The next few years saw him drifting across the wide expanse of the south-west cattle country. As a jobbing cow-hand he could never settle in one place for more than a season, always searching for that fabled *El Dorado* that might just materialize beyond the next horizon.

Then it happened. Just by chance.

Caught in the middle of a range war up in Montana, he had discovered that wealthy ranchers were prepared to pay good money for a man who knew which end of a gun did the killing. And being a paid gun-hand was much more rewarding than punching cows from dawn 'til dusk, and a much easier proposition to boot.

But Largo had never cottoned to being given orders. He preferred to do things his own way. So long as the job got done, it didn't matter to him that maybe a few extra dead bodies was the result. His ruthless pursuance of an objective left him with a reputation that many potential employers feared. They wanted the job done, just so long as it left them untainted, their respectability within the community firmly intact.

Men like Largo were unpredictable, too hot-headed. Independent spirits who answered to no one.

Too many killings were difficult to explain away.

And Largo was a man of few words, a man who spoke with a cocked .45. Early on in life he had learned that a fast, accurate gun hand was worth a thousand words. Jawing had no place when obstacles of the human variety needed removing. Unlike some other gunslicks of his ilk, Largo had never enjoyed killing. It was just a lucrative way of making an easy living. And the more notches that were carved into the grip of his shooter, the easier it became.

Not that he lacked principles. It had never been his way to eradicate those he considered innocent victims of some unscrupulous rancher's greedy whim.

There was that time back in '72 when a Wyoming cattle man had hired him to get rid of a family of nesters who were supposedly blocking his access to water. Largo accepted half payment of the thousand dollar fee in advance. Jake Farlow employed over twenty hands on the Flying F and had built a sumptuous ranch house high on a rocky knoll overlooking Thunder Basin in the north of the state.

He had everything.

When Largo rode out to investigate the so-called impediment to further extension of the rancher's holding, he discovered a family scrabbling desperately to make ends meet. The small two-roomed soddy with its dirt floor was home to a family of four. Farlow had already tried unsuccessfully to scare the nesters off by destroying their corn crop: now he had instructed Largo to burn them out.

Further investigation indicated there was water enough for everybody in the valley. Greed and power were the rancher's prime motivating forces. He wanted to be the kingpin. And Largo despised such men.

So, instead of carrying out orders, he acted completely out of character by handing over his fee to the impoverished farmer. To ensure there was no adverse retribution against the nesters, he returned to the Flying F ranch house that night and left a note pinned to the carcass of Farlow's prize bull. It read: *Should any harm come to Treat Williams and his family, I will return. Largo.*

Nothing else. Farlow would understand. The hired gun was nothing if true to his word. Such was his reputation.

That was how Largo became an unofficial law enforcement representative.

One of a breed which was despised throughout the western frontier territories, the bounty killer was feared even more by those whom he hunted down. Killers and road agents with a price on their heads knew that sooner or later, men like Largo would come a-calling, and with all guns blazing.

Official agents of the law hated these hired guns with a vengeance, mainly because they operated independently. Strict rules existed regarding collection of reward payouts. And lawmen had to forego that pleasure. For many, it was a pill that was exceedingly hard to swallow.

Now in his middle thirties, Largo was at a stage in life where he was considered at the peak of his profession. And for a man who hunted down others for a living, the only way forward was downhill. Sooner or later as he grew older, and slower on the draw, some young gunny would chance his hand, and have the edge. All that was needed was a split second to put him out of action for good.

For the bounty-hunter, there was no easing down of the reins, no sitting back like some bank teller waiting on his retirement pension. Largo knew that only too well. But he was hooked: the excitement of the chase; the tightness in his chest when an opponent stood his ground; payoff time.

Dead or Alive. That's what the posters read.

It was up to the bad ass to decide. It was his funeral — Boot Hill or the Pen. Largo preferred them dead — easier to handle. But he always gave them the option. Live or die. Nobody could accuse him of being anything but fair.

It was a dangerous profession, but one that had netted him a sizeable pot over the years. Resting in the bank at El Paso lay a grubstake of no mean proportions. Largo reckoned that in another few months he would have amassed sufficient *dinero* to buy himself a decent spread back in his home state of Texas.

Until then, he would have to continue in the business of man-hunting.

2

Wanted

For the past hour since cresting the pass over Antelope Ridge, Largo's dust-caked eyes had remained firmly set on the distant outline of the west-bound railroad. Now, little more than a mile distant, he could just pick out a round dark object on the platform. It hovered in the undulating heat waves, then disappeared inside the wooden building.

That would be Henry Tasker, the depot clerk. Enquiries from the station master at Hobbs had revealed some interesting information.

The rail depot at Carlsbad Junction was where the county sheriff sent the latest batch of wanted dodgers relating to the southern half of New Mexico. Freight carriers then distributed them around the territory. And Tasker was deeply in debt to the bank for money borrowed to buy a new house in Buckeye where he lived. Being the sole employee on the Southern Pacific payroll at Carlsbad, Largo foresaw no problems in persuading the official to let him peruse the batch.

Anybody short on the readies was a ripe plum to be picked as far as Largo was concerned. He smiled mirthlessly. This visit could prove to be very profitable.

'Yessiree, Dancer old gal,' smirked Largo, stroking the pointed ears of the grey, 'This jigger could supply us with a few choice jobs if my info is correct.' The rough drawl laced with a Texan burr made the horse snicker in accord. Dancer lifted her front legs in the characteristic prance that had captured Largo's heart whilst passing through Durango the previous fall.

His mount at the time was suffering badly from weak muscles and strained tendons. Not surprising since Blanco was well past retirement age as far as horses were concerned. He had sold the old feller to a wrangler who said the ageing cayuse would be ideal for his kids.

Wandering through the Colorado mining camp, Largo had chanced upon a grim scenario that had made his blood boil. A recalcitrant miner had taken a whip to the grey mare he was trying to mount. Too much liquor at the local saloon was no excuse for such vile treatment. Snorting and caterwauling the feisty horse had taken umbrage at the brutal assault she was receiving. Largo had likewise been piqued to witness such a fine animal being so roughly handled.

On voicing his disquiet in no uncertain terms, the soused varmint had foolishly gone for his gun. Not a sound decision where a guy like Largo was concerned. Luckily the town marshal had witnessed the incident and knew that the stranger had been given little choice in the matter. Nonetheless he was quick to recognize a lethal bounty killer in their midst. His advice, firmly administered, was for Largo to move on at the earliest opportunity.

He did so the next day in the company of his new mount.

The horse whinnied, automatically upping the pace to a canter. She had sensed the smell of water.

A warm breeze sprang up as Largo neared the junction. The steady draught stirred the torrid air nudging the well pump into motion. Lack of grease made it squeal as the underground spring water was sucked upwards into the wooden tower.

After tying off the grey, Largo pushed the door of the depot office, instinctively stepping back a pace before entering. It was a precaution that had saved his hide on more than one occasion. You never could tell what was waiting behind an unknown door.

'Come on in, stranger,' offered the depot clerk rising to his feet. 'Take the weight off your legs and wet your whistle. Only got bottled beer, mind.' A broad smile creased the florid visage. It wasn't often that Henry Tasker had company. 'Come far?' he asked, pouring the tepid beer into a glass.

Largo's hooded gaze surveyed every nook and cranny before responding. Even then it was curt and brief.

'Some.' The reply elicited an irritated grunt from Tasker. He wanted two-way dialogue. Five days' jawing to yourself was apt to jangle a man's brain cells.

'If you're hopin' to catch the west-bound train, then you're a hour late,' persisted Tasker sipping at his own drink. 'Next one ain't 'til noon tomorrer.'

Largo accepted the proffered glass and drank long and deep. Even warm beer was welcome after five days on the trail. He wiped his lips on the sleeve of his grey flannel shirt holding the other man's curious gaze.

'You are here fer the train, ain't yer?' pressed Tasker somewhat diffidently. This jasper was beginning to make him

19

a mite edgy. That tied-down Colt low on the big guy's right hip didn't help. Fellers who wore their irons that away usually intended it for a reason. Ordinary cowpunchers off the range often didn't even carry a gun on their person. 'Cos there ain't nothin' else around here.' Then he added, a little too quickly, 'Don't keep no cash on the premises neither.'

A gentle smile creased the newcomer's craggy face. Largo flipped a cigar butt from his vest pocket with one hand, scratching a vesta down the office wall with the other. Blue smoke drifted from between thin lips obscuring the piercing regard from grey eyes that stared intently.

Tasker waited, his fingers drumming nervously on the desk top. More beads of sweat popped on his bald dome giving him a shiny, almost polished hue.

'Might be here to catch the train,' offered Largo eventually. He took another haul on the cigar. 'Depends.'

'On what?' croaked Tasker.

Largo's icy gaze narrowed beneath the brim of his hat.

'On whether you're gonna be co-operative.'

'Co-operative?' Tasker's response was a tight squawk. He swallowed hard.

'My information is that every month you get a bunch of new wanted posters sent down from Roswell. The train conductor drops them off at stops along the line.'

The bounty-hunter paused to let the import of his words sink in. Then he took out a bundle of notes and slowly peeled off fifty dollars and placed it on the table in front of the gaping clerk. Casually but with mindful intent, his right hand toyed with the Colt. In the flick of a rattler's tongue, the gun leapt into his right hand. A deft spin on the middle finger, then back into the greased leather holster.

'Get my drift, mister?'

Tasker blinked. His jaw scraped on the floor.

'Erm . . . th-these here posters are

21

meant for the eyes of town marshals only,' he stammered, one eye on the visitor, the other avidly creaming off the pile of greenbacks. The mortgage of his new house was far more than the meagre wages of a depot clerk could handle.

Largo's fervid gaze hardened.

'I could allus just help myself,' he said evenly. His hand strayed towards the cash.

Quick as lightning, the clerk grabbed up the dough and opened the top drawer of the desk. Inside was a large brown envelope which he lifted out and handed to Largo.

The bounty-hunter smiled. The look was one of arrogant disdain. Then he opened the package and began to scrutinize the contents.

The first three were for peanuts. Petty thieves stealing from general stores. He was after the big boys, those worthy of pursuit. Rough House Charlie Sinclair was wanted for bank robbery with a price of $500 on his head. Scanning the details, however, revealed that he would have to be delivered to Tucson in Arizona territory.

Much too far. He wanted something close by.

And he knew that Black Bergis and his gang had been captured by Texas Rangers over in Amarillo. That left Hambone Walker. Wanted in two states and the territory of New Mexico for a double murder and numerous stage hold-ups; $800. Last known hangout: *Alamagordo*.

A stubby forefinger prodded the ugly pen drawing of his next job.

'Hambone Walker,' murmured Largo to himself. 'I'm acomin' to get yuh!'

Removing the rest of the posters for Hambone Walker, Largo struck another vesta and consigned them to oblivion. No sense in giving the opposition an even break. Largo knew that any bounty-hunter worth his salt would take every opportunity to outwit the opposition. On more than one occasion he had hunted down good paying rewards only to find they had already been claimed. In one case only hours before.

Grinding the blackened ashes under his boot, he said, 'These posters never arrived at Carlsbad Junction. Right, mister?'

Tasker nodded. He was quite prepared to bend the rules for a rake off, but did not want any nosy railroad official suspecting him of feeding information to bounty-hunters. 'You won't say where you got the lowdown, will yuh?' pleaded Tasker pushing another bottle towards his visitor.

Largo wasn't listening. Now he had the whip hand.

Alamagordo next stop!

He stuffed the lone poster into his pocket.

'Be seeing you again next month.' Before the depot clerk knew what was happening, Largo's ham-like fist shot out and pinned him to the wall. His next words were issued in a low hiss, laced with overt menace, 'And if anybody should happen to discover our little arrangement, make no mistake, I'll be back. And feeding your mangy hide to the buzzards will be reward enough for me.'

Unceremoniously, he pushed the quaking tub of lard into his chair and clumped out onto the empty platform. A high-pitched whistle summoned Dancer from a juicy patch of grass beneath the leaking water tower.

The sun was pitching down towards the western horizon throwing elongated shadows across the bleak terrain. Largo's objective lay on the far side of the Sacramento Mountains. There was another three hours before sundown. Time enough to reach the foothills and make camp for the night.

He tweaked the grey's ears, well satisfied with the outcome of his visit to Carlsbad Junction. Dancer could sense her master's pleasure. Proud head bobbing, she instantly picked up the pace towards the distant range of mountains.

3

Alamagordo

It was four days later that man and beast reached the edge of a high mesa overlooking Alamagordo. Largo nudged the grey down through a gap in the fractured sandstone wall. Picking a delicate path among the heaps of red detritus, he eventually gained the desert floor and was able to spur forward along an arrow-straight trail. The town simmered in the early afternoon heat. It nestled in a depression to the east of a rolling plain of pure white sand which stretched uninterrupted all the way to the distant San Andreas range.

Hauling rein on the edge of the small cluster of wooden buildings, Largo surveyed this sorry excuse for a town. None of the clapboard structures appeared to have been given a lick of paint for some considerable time. Where colour did impinge itself on his retina, it was flaky and blistering. Bleached by the pulsating heat, false-fronted buildings despondently lined the single street; the only attempt at decoration being hand-painted signs advertising the occupant's trade. All that is except the bank. A solid brick structure, it stood out like a sore thumb.

What sort of a place was this? Nobody on the street. Not even a dog chasing its traditional enemy. Maybe they were all taking a siesta. After all, this was New Mexico.

Then a red sign caught his eye — Painted Lady Saloon. He could sure use a glass of cool beer, froth bubbling over the side of the glass. The thought made Largo's leathery tongue rasp against his equally dry lips. His last water had been used to boil up a pot of coffee that morning.

Dancer's grey head sagged under the relentless pounding from above. Then she sniffed, one eye swinging towards a water trough outside the saloon. Three other mounts were already slaking their fill. Without further hesitation, Dancer joined them.

Tying off at the hitching rail, Largo nodded to the astute horse.

'You sure have cottoned to the right notion there, old gal,' he affirmed with a knowing smile as he made to enter the drinking den. 'Got me a thirst more rampant than a desert camel.'

Not only that but he knew from past experience that bartenders knew everything that went on in a town, sometimes even before it happened. The plank door squeaked on rusted hinges. Not a good sign. Pausing just inside but without offering a tempting silhouette to any trigger-happy rannie who might be on the lam, he allowed his eyes to become accustomed to the gloom.

Sawdust covered the dirt floor to mop up any spilt liquid. It badly needed changing if the smell was anything to go by. The usual assortment of drinkers who frequented such establishments were idly lounging against the bar. Range hands in leather chaps stood hunched over their glasses. At a green baize table sat a nattily attired dude sporting a black derby, clearly the house gambler. At that moment he was idly playing patience all on his lonesome. A girl was conversing with the resident pianist. Other nondescripts appeared to offer no threat.

Satisfied, Largo sidled up to the bar and slapped a silver dollar on the counter.

The scruffy barfly ignored the newcomer, continuing his conversation with a dark-suited jasper.

Largo was prepared to wait. But not for long.

'You servin', or is this a help-yourself?'

The barkeep deigned to raise a bushy eyebrow, his thick fleshy lip curled in a lurid scowl. A potentially lucrative business meeting was more important

29

than some no-account range bum.

'In a minute,' he rasped impatiently, returning his attention to the interrupted discourse.

Two minutes passed. Then Largo pushed himself off the counter and slid round the side of the bar. Selecting a large tankard, he opened the beer tap and let it gush onto the floor. This immediately had the full attention of the barman.

'What the hell you doin'?'

'You ain't servin'. So I'm helpin' myself.'

'That ain't allowed.'

'It is now.'

The barfly's round face turned a tawdry shade of purple. Veins like thick string pulsated on his stocky neck.

'And what about all that beer?'

'What about it?'

'It's all goin' to waste.'

'Need me a cooling drink. Not that tepid muck still in the pipes.'

'It'll be cool enough by now.'

The guy's nose was twitching. In fact

his whole body was shaking. He was panicking. The shotgun he kept hidden for emergencies was secreted under the bar counter, but out of reach on the far side of this trespassing critter.

Largo's craggy features split in a broad smile. He was enjoying himself.

'In a minute,' he opined, consciously dipping his fingers into the foaming beer and slurping the liquid with the supposed aim of testing the temperature. 'Yep. Another minute should do it.'

'OK, mister,' a grating voice barked from the doorway, 'You've had yer fun.'

Largo swung to face the speaker. The sun reflected off the five-pointed tin star of the town marshal. A large bulky jigger wearing Levis and a sheepskin jacket filled the doorway. More important was the .44 Remington six-shooter in his left hand. And it was pointing at Largo's head.

'Might I suggest that you return to this side of the bar' — the words were uttered in a casual rather flippant tone, but the underlying menace was evident should they be ignored — 'where I am sure Moonshine will be more than happy to serve you.' Then he added for the benefit of the bartender known throughout the county as Moonshine Morgan, 'And I'm sure that the gentleman would appreciate a smile and a friendly greeting to accompany his drink.' An eyebrow lifted knowingly towards the squirming Morgan.

'Sure, Marshal. No problem.' The surly reply had to be dragged up from the barman's bulging stomach.

Having no wish to antagonize the local lawdog, Largo turned off the beer tap and did as requested.

'OK with you?' The marshal's question was addressed to Largo.

The bounty-hunter tipped his hat to the lawman who had carefully noted the gleaming Colt Frontier complete with its cut-down rig.

Chet Ramage knew the breed. Jiggers who hired their skill to the highest bidder, although this fellow appeared to have a looser, more relaxed manner about him than most other gunfighters he had come across. In the marshal's view, he didn't immediately spell trouble. Not yet anyway. And Ramage prided himself on being a connoisseur when it came to human nature.

'Now that you've made the beer nice and cold, maybe you would have one with me?' he offered, returning his own iron to its holster and stepping up to the bar.

'Much obliged, Marshal.'

'Could be you've started a new trend,' Ramage declared pointedly, aiming the remark towards Moonshine Morgan. 'Cold beer in the Painted Lady? Never happened before.'

Largo sank his tankard in a single draught, sighing contentedly as he wiped his lips with the back of his hand.

'That sure hit the mark and no mistake,' he professed.

Ramage was studying him closely over his half-filled pot.

'You got a handle then, mister?'

A pause as the stranger held the other's gaze.

'The name's Largo,' he murmured. The eyes were cold and dark. Deep set pools that gave nothing away.

The tin star visibly stiffened, his hand automatically sliding down to rest on the pistol butt.

'Seems like I've heard that name before.'

'He's a bounty killer, Marshal,' piped up Moonshine Morgan, pleased that the unwelcome attention had passed to the newcomer. 'They say he allus brings 'em in draped over a saddle.'

'Just doin' a public service is all,' countered Largo. He suddenly felt he had to justify himself to this representative of the law.

'You visitin' Alamagordo on business then, Mr Largo?' enquired the marshal. 'Or just passin' through?'

'Ain't quite decided yet.' Questions were anathema to men in Largo's profession. Especially from lawdogs.

'So what's gonna make up your mind?'

'Depends on whether there's business for me to conduct in this here town.'

Ramage nodded, set his hat straight, then headed for the door. He knew the score.

'Nice drinking with you Mr Largo,' he said, then stopped and swung on his heel. 'The kind of business you're in,' — Ramage narrowed his eyes resting them on the bounty-hunter — 'I try to run a quiet town. And plan to keep it that way. *Comprendez?*'

'Do my best, Marshal. But some jiggers allus wanna argue the point.'

Ramage scowled but had to be content with that.

Largo turned towards the barman who once again became the object of attention. Morgan fidgeted with a towel, then said, 'You heard the marshal. He don't want no trouble in Alamagordo.' The barman's mouth twitched nervously at the corners as he muttered, 'And far as I know, there ain't no bad asses in this town.'

Slowly, Largo removed the poster of Hambone Walker from his jacket and laid it flat on the counter facing the barfly.

'Know him?' he hissed.

'N-never s-seen him.' Morgan's teeth were chattering, and not with the cold. He had not even looked at the poster.

In a single fluid motion, Largo reached across the bar and grabbed Morgan by the shirt front. Buttons popped as the hatchet-faced 'keep panted in fear. A palpable silence had settled over the room. The other drinkers were now more intent on the action taking place at the bar.

'Now I'll ask you again.' The daunting undertone from Largo was all the more menacing due to its flat delivery. This and the .45 prodding Morgan's red snout persuaded the barman to lower his gaze to the poster.

'Well?'

Their eyes met. Blood drained from Morgan's visage. Then his gaze slowly lifted. Largo's followed.

So. Hambone Walker was closer than he had ever imagined.

Releasing the trembling beer puller, Largo emphasized his next words with the cold hard barrel of the .45 jammed in the poor dude's open mouth.

'Now I'm a-goin' upstairs. And you're stayin' down here to serve the customers. Any warning to old Hambone and it's . . . ' — the hammer on the Colt clicked back — 'bang, bang. Goodbye, Mr Moonshine! Got that?'

Morgan crapped his pants. He had gotten the message.

★　★　★

At the top of the stairs, Largo's sharp eye homed in onto the only door that was closed. It lay at the far end of a dimly lit corridor on the right. That had to be the one where Hambone Walker was in residence. Facing him, a window opened onto a balcony overlooking the main street. Largo afforded himself a perceptive nod. Sidling cat-like to the far end of the corridor, he lifted up the sash to its full extent, careful to avoid any harsh squeak.

With the .45 palmed, he flicked out the ejector gate to check the load. As expected, the revolver needed a sixth cartridge which he quickly inserted. Leathering the pistol, he unrolled the all-important poster and padded charily towards the closed door.

Ears attuned to every little nuance of sound, he filtered out the muted babble from below, concentrating on the upstairs room. The clink of steel cutlery told him that Walker was enjoying a meal; no doubt his favourite pork, bacon and corn dodgers. Before joining the owlhoot trail, the wanted outlaw had reared pigs back in his home state of Missouri.

Satisfied that his quarry was in the room, Largo tensed, then slid the flattened poster under the door.

He held his breath, the lean body rock steady.

He didn't have long to wait for the

expected reaction. A puzzled grunt was followed by a low snarl, then the clattering of discarded cutlery.

Largo quickly retreated to the balcony. Three shots blasted one after the other ripping through the thin wooden door where he had been standing seconds before. Without bothering to determine whether his aim had been successful, the fugitive emerged from his room window onto the balcony. His horse was below, ready for a quick getaway in case just such an eventuality as this occurred.

'Goin' somewhere, Hambone?'

The brittle question brought the outlaw up short. He froze, right hand hovering above his holstered gun.

'Now just raise your hands, and come peaceful like,' said Largo, pointing his shooter at the outlaw. 'I ain't never shot a man in the back.' He paused emitting a gruff chortle. 'But there's allus a first time for everything.'

Walker was shaking. Should he take the chance? He'd done it before. A diving swing to the left, draw and fire. That deputy over in Chaves County hadn't known what had hit him. Then again, this guy sounded awful sure of himself.

'So what's it to be, pig brain?' scoffed Largo egging the guy on. He wasn't that keen on live subjects. They meant trouble. 'Live or die!'

Oh! What the hell!

Walker pirouetted lithely, just like a ballet dancer. He made to dive left. The gun was halfway out of its holster when he was slammed back against the balcony rails as two chunks of hot lead ploughed into his chest. Plumb centre, just a whisker apart. Walker's mouth drooped, a trickle of blood seeping from the corners. His rapidly glazing eyes studied the red stuff pulsating from the fatal wounds.

Once again, the Frontier spoke as another shell pumped into the sagging torso. The shot was enough to knock the outlaw's punctured frame over the low railing. It hit the awning that covered the boardwalk, then rolled over to land with a dull thud in the street below. A rusty stain spilled across the sand beneath the lifeless corpse.

'Too bad, Hambone,' muttered the bounty-hunter holstering his own weapon. 'You made the wrong choice.'

Down in the street, a crowd had gathered round the still body. Even though the marshal claimed to maintain law and order, in truth death was no stranger to Alamagordo — reason enough why any termination was met with nervous trepidation by the morbid voyeurs. They could be next in line to shake hands with the grim reaper.

'Step aside and let me through.'

Marshal Ramage's gruff retort instantly parted the murmuring crowd.

'Who did this?' he snapped, looking around at the sea of blank faces. Puzzled shrugs and a shaking of heads met his questioning glower.

'That's my doin', Marshal,' announced Largo, stepping into the circle that surrounded the grim scene. Without waiting for any comeback, he produced the wanted dodger and handed it to Ramage. 'Hambone Walker, wanted for a heap of criminal activity, and with a price of eight hundred bucks on his head.' He paused, levelling a steady eye on the lawman. 'Dead or alive! He chose dead.'

Ramage snatched the poster, briefly scanned it, then grunted.

'Thought I told you to keep that smokepole leathered.'

'Not my fault, Marshal,' Largo shrugged, raising his hands in mock surrender. 'I gave him the option. He chose wrong.'

'Well I ain't gotten that kind of dough to hand,' said Ramage brusquely. 'Take a week for it to arrive from Roswell.'

'I can wait,' drawled Largo, extracting another half-smoked butt and lighting up. Then to the crowd he asked, 'Anybody recommend a good eating-house for a hungry traveller?'

'Mary Jane'll fix you some victuals,' piped up an old-timer. 'Best steaks this side of El Paso.'

Largo acknowledged the speaker then added, 'Will one of you kind folks see to my horse?'

'No problem,' squealed a young kid, pushing through the jostling throng. 'My pa runs the best livery in town.'

Largo smiled, nonchalantly flipping a silver dollar at the scrawny urchin. 'Keep the change, kid.'

'Gee thanks, mister,' grinned the youngster, leading Dancer away and staring wide-eyed at the large gleaming coin.

'Seems like you got a right friendly town here, Marshal,' observed Largo, swinging his saddle-bag over the right shoulder. 'Maybe I could be tempted to stay on more'n a week.'

Ramage scowled but said nothing. The black moustache bristled. He was beginning to have grave doubts about befriending this rannigan. Bounty-hunters were always bad news. This feller was becoming something of a hero. Sooner that reward arrived from Roswell the better he'd feel.

4

The Red River Five

It was three days later that a heavy knock sounded on the marshal's door.

Looking up from his paperwork, Ramage grunted impatiently. Gone were the days when a peace-officer's duty was to carry out the letter of the law, arrest the perpetrators and send them before the court. Now it was endless reports, forms and electioneering. He hadn't signed up to be no pen-pushing clerk. Nor some politician touting for his own job. Time was when all a feller needed were a solid pair of fists, a clear head and to know his way around a gun.

Ramage shook his head in exasperation and threw the pen onto the desk. A large blot smudged his latest offering to head office.

'Goldarnit!' he yammered, slamming back his chair. 'Come in if you have to. The door's open.'

It was Largo.

'Heard anythin' about that reward yet, Marshal?' he asked, biting the end off a cigar. 'Time I was uppin' stakes. Hear tell there could be some'n for me over in Silver City. Young tearaway by the name of Bonney seems to be tryin' to make a name fer hisself.'

The news that Ramage's unwelcome guest was after leaving Alamagordo was like a breath of fresh air. The marshal quickly simmered down and offered his visitor a mug of coffee. At the same time he placed a lighted vesta to the brown tube clutched between Largo's clenched teeth.

Blue smoke spiralled in the dusty atmosphere.

'You'll get yer money, never fret,' replied the marshal, sipping his own drink. 'It's bin approved by the county sheriff's office. Should be here in four maybe five days.' He strode across to a

45

noticeboard, prodding at a poster. 'This here's the guy yer after,' he said. 'William H. Bonney otherwise known as Billy the Kid.' The marshal's bent snout wrinkled. 'Nasty piece of goods by all accounts. Like as not to haul off at the drop of a hat.'

Largo peered at the reward on offer. That was more of interest to him than the Kid's temperament.

'Four hundred, is that all?' he scoffed 'Don't seem worth the bother. Maybe I'll stick around Alamagordo. Nice town.'

Ramage's brow lifted, his broad back stiffened. This was not what he wanted to hear. Rapidly his keen eye scanned the poster's small print below the pen drawing of the scowling gunslinger. A sharp intake of breath was accompanied by fierce jabbing at the all-important paragraph.

'There!' he barked with a gravelly chuckle. 'Last seen in Lincoln. That's no more'n two days' ride through the Ruidoso Range. And it says here that the reward is negotiable. Feller in your line could easily up the ante by a good two hundred bucks.' Ramage stood grinning, hands on hips. 'Nothin' round here worth hangin' about fer. You could be there 'n back with the reward waitin' on yer, and an extra profit to boot.'

'Maybe.' Largo's reply was loose, cautious. 'Maybe not.' He was giving nothing away. Tipping his hat, he turned to leave. 'I'll be at the Longhorn if'n you need me.' Clean straw and an exotic floor show had persuaded Largo to opt for Alamagordo's other saloon.

Ramage sighed, turning back to his hated paperwork. Blasted bounty-hunter. Why couldn't he make up his mind, and just leave. Seems like the jasper enjoyed keeping lawmen on a string.

Following a hearty lunch at Mary Jane's Diner, Largo decided to take the marshal's advice. No sense in hanging around this no-account berg twiddling his thumbs. Might just as well see if he could make some extra dough.

Mounting Dancer, who had been

thoroughly enjoying herself at the livery stable during his absence, he headed north to visit the town of Lincoln. Perhaps this Bonney Kid would still be around. In any case, it never did any harm to check out potential 'clients' before making their acquaintance. And this young gunslinger seemed like a new breed that drew down just for the hell of it.

Around the same time as Largo was pulling out, five dusty riders drew to a halt on a flat piece of high ground to the south of Alamagordo. Could be they even noticed the rider on a grey mare heading north. Whatever, they paid him no heed.

'You sure this bank is gonna be a pushover?' hissed Mangas Pete, tipping a flat plainsman to the back of his bony skull to obtain a better look. He was a small weasel of a guy, insipid and pale in appearance, but deadly accurate with a throwing knife. When silence was needed, Pete was your man.

Texas Jack Cantrell uttered an

exasperated sigh.

'Ain't I told yer a dozen times already? The safe is chock full of greenbacks at this time of the month. Tomorrow is payday for the miners. But today is gonna be payday for the Red River Gang.'

Mangas sniffed. 'Just askin' is all.'

Cautious and distrusting, that was Mangas Pete. Not that Cantrell minded. In fact, he preferred guys who were thus disposed to hot heads like Rufe Claybourne, although the little runt's constant whinging could get a mite wearing at times.

Immediately behind Cantrell, Chero-kee George rode silent as always. Straight-backed and vigilant, he was the product of a white mother who had been taken captive by the tribe when she was little more than a child. George had learned the tracking skills that made him a boon to the gang from his father, a full-blood Cherokee chieftain and expert marksman with a longbow. His son was equally adept, but had gravitated to the latest repeating rifles with which he was no less accomplished.

Slim Brewster was a lean hard-bitten desperado. He had only recently joined the gang following a bank raid at the town of Socorro which had resulted in the unfortunate loss of Cantrell's second in command.

The capture of Dogface Mendoza had depressed him. The Mexican gunslinger was worth half-a-dozen ordinary lawbreakers. He had been found guilty of murder and robbery and been sentenced to hang at Fort Sumner. The bounty on his head was now wiped clean.

'How come this town has so much dough?' enquired a large ungainly rannie, butting in on Cantrell's mordant thoughts. Rufe Claybourne was heavy set with a black beard and matching long hair spilling from beneath a high-crowned sombrero. 'It don't seem much from up here.'

His pox-riddled visage bent in a

lop-sided grimace.

Cantrell didn't answer. His hawkish gaze was sweeping the arid terrain, searching; making certain that no reception party was awaiting their arrival.

Eventually he spoke.

'Alamagordo is the collection point for four mining camps.'

'How come it ain't never been done before then?' pressed Claybourne. He was a mean-eyed gunslick, hard of face and equally ruthless when it came to gunplay. Having killed five men that Cantrell was aware of, the reward on his head had now topped a grand, only $300 less than the gang boss himself.

Cantrell uttered a manic cackle. He shifted the black hat to the back of his head. 'That's why I'm the leader of this outfit see, Rufe.' His response was low and even in tone. 'It's me that has the brains, and does all the organizing.'

Claybourne stirred, his ugly face creasing into a snarl.

'You got a problem with that?' spat

the gang leader, holding the other man with a rock steady glare. Sooner or later he felt there was going to be a showdown between them. And Texas Jack intended walking away from that one unscathed, and maybe drawing on that reward.

The gunman balked but knew his place. He was no leader, but it irked him to be reminded of that fact. One day Cantrell would go too far. But he said nothing. Gnarled hands flexed convulsively then relaxed.

The gang boss snorted triumphantly then shifted his attention to the town's main drag. He flipped out his time-piece. It read four o'clock in the afternoon.

'Bank closes in thirty minutes,' he announced. 'The best time to strike. No customers, tellers ready to call it a day, and the safe full to bursting.' He emitted a hearty guffaw. Then, in a more serious vein, 'OK boys, check your weapons are fully loaded and ready for action.'

Hammers clicked, cylinders twirled as fresh shells were injected into an array of side arms and rifles. Satisfied, Cantrell nudged the blue roan forward at the canter. The others fell in behind. Five dark shadows etched starkly against the blanched whiteness of the desert.

★　★　★

'Ready to lock up for the day, Miss Challener?' enquired the bank manager.

Herman Jeffrey was a small portly gent. Florid of visage and smooth cheeked, his round face gave the appearance of a rosy apple. He was a fussy, rather prim individual who insisted that every last cent be accounted for in the daily ledger.

Jane Challener flicked a long curly tress from her pale face and nodded.

'What time will the mining payrolls be handed over?' she asked, carefully placing the large leather-backed ledger files in a cupboard. 'I am always so relieved when all that money has been transferred.'

'No need to worry. The mining agents should be here around noon tomorrow,' replied Jeffrey, buttoning his top coat before adjusting the black silk hat at a jaunty angle. Peering into his mirror, he gave a haughty sniff of admiration.

'Are you going straight home, erm . . . Jane?' This latter query was uttered in a rather halting voice. The familiarity was uncertain, lacking confidence. Herman Jeffrey was not what could be termed a lady's man. He had the power, the money, but lacked those all-important qualities for a potential Lothario — good looks and a sense of humour.

Miss Challener was used to these blundering attempts by her boss to place their relationship on a more personal footing. Each time she made some excuse without causing offence. After all, her job was at stake. And a single lady needed her independence.

'I regret so, Mr Jeffrey,' she replied firmly. 'My mother is awaiting me with supper on the table.'

'Perhaps another time.'

'Perhaps.'

That was when the never-changing daily routine at the bank slipped from its regular course. The door opened and four men walked in.

'I am sorry, gentlemen,' intoned the bank manager pompously, 'but the bank is now closed for the day. We will be open again at nine sharp in the morning.'

That should have been it. A brief acknowledgement from the late-comers and then exit the premises. These four stayed put, unshifting in their stance.

'We won't be here tomorrow,' retorted the tall man dressed in black corduroys and a leather vest. His face was hidden beneath a dust-caked stetson. 'And neither will the contents of that there safe.' Instantly, four Colt revolvers appeared in four hands. 'Now fill these sacks with them greenbacks,' stated the big man with a biting inflection. 'This is a hold-up.'

Miss Challener screamed.

'Stow that caterwaulin', yer crazy female,' snapped an ugly little runt boasting a livid scar down his cheek. 'Else I'll cut out yer liver.' The snub-nosed .36 wagging provocatively was matched by the glinting steel of a lethal stiletto.

'Now be a good girl and do as the boss tells yuh,' added a third man gruffly.

'And hurry it up,' barked the leader stepping forward and jamming the barrel of his pistol viciously into the quivering belly of Herman Jeffrey. The manager sank to the floor, gasping for breath and clutching his injured middle. He had never been involved with robbers before and shock had taken possession of his inert limbs.

'Leave him be,' wailed Jane Challener rushing to his aid. 'Can't you see the poor man needs help?'

'He'll get a dose of lead poisoning

if'n he don't cough up the safe key,' rapped the gang leader, his boot connecting with Jeffrey's ribs.

This caused a fresh outburst from the panicking girl.

'Someone shut her up,' yelled Brewster waving his pistol.

Not used to ladies of a more delicate persuasion, Rufe Claybourne lost his cool. His temper had always been of a less than calm disposition. Now a red mist drifted across his crazed features. Growling like an injured bear, his gun erupted. In the confined space, the noise was brutally sadistic. Two heavy .44 shells gut-busted the screaming girl slamming her against the wall.

Slowly, she slid down the wall leaving a smear of bright red behind. A crimson stream dribbled from her mouth which hung open like a broken door. Brown eyes, once brimming with youthful exuberance, glazed over, blank and lifeless.

'You danged fool,' jabbered Cantrell, 'What d'yuh go and do that fer?'

'Stupid bitch was goin' crazy,' burbled Claybourne in his defence.

'Too damn late now,' rapped Cantrell desperately searching the blubbering bank manager's pockets for the all-important key. Luckily it was soon to hand. Cantrell was nothing if not cool under pressure. Quickly he issued fresh orders. No sense squawking over spilt milk. Time enough for recriminations later.

The large wall clock ticked ominously.

'Mangas!' he rapped. 'You join Cherokee outside. Keep any bravehearts at bay.'

The little man needed no second bidding. He rushed outside.

Cantrell's next brittle command was to Claybourne and Brewster.

'You two help me get these bags filled.'

There were five sacks in all. Halfway through the fourth sack, he heard a panicky shout from outside.

'Someone get the marshal! The bank's being robbed!'

Gunfire immediately erupted in the street. Cantrell realized it was time they were elsewhere. But like all *bandidos*, he hated leaving anything behind.

'Outside!' he snapped at his two sidekicks, 'I'll finish off here.' Rufe hesitated. 'Git goin',' snarled the gang boss, spearing the hard ass with an ugly stare.

The man known as Brewster plucked at Claybourne's arm. 'This ain't the time fer no blasted arguments,' he yelled, as a window shattered inwards showering them with splinters of glass. A brief struggle with his fiery temper then Rufe Claybourne followed the retreating outlaw.

Cantrell hurriedly completed the task of filling the sacks with paper money. He ignored the loose change that lay scattered across the wooden floor like wedding confetti. Urgency to quit the scene was indelibly written across the lined face as the gun battle outside the bank intensified. Bullets slammed into the brick walls. More windows splintered. Dogs joined in the frenetic mayhem, howling mournfully.

A cry of pain lanced through the general cacophony. Had one of his own men been hit? He had no way of knowing.

But he had one last card up his sleeve.

Grabbing the snuffling bank manager, he growled, 'On yer feet, fat ass. You're coming with us.'

Jeffrey howled as he was manhandled to his feet and hustled out of the door.

'W-where are you taking me?'

Cantrell ignored the tremulous enquiry, his giant paw firmly gripping the coat collar of the quivering wreck.

In the street, two of the town's citizens lay dead.

'Mount up, boys,' shouted Cantrell, through the pall of gun smoke that twirled in the charged atmosphere.

At that moment Marshal Ramage stepped from behind a buggy immediately to the left of the bank. His pistol roared twice.

Brewster threw up his arms and fell to the boardwalk.

'No thievin' skunks are gonna rob a bank in my town,' rasped the lawman, stepping forward. 'Now throw down your weapons.'

Unseen by the advancing lawman, Mangas Pete was hidden by a thick veranda support. Thin lips drew back in a mirthless grin. Then with deft precision and an uncanny accuracy he launched his deadly blade. Ramage never saw it coming. He spun round in a full circle grabbing at the hilt protruding from his left shoulder.

Cantrell gave a whoop of triumph.

'That's the way to treat a tin star,' he smirked, congratulating his sidekick. Then to the threatening townsfolk, 'Now listen up, you turkeys. Anyone tries to stop us gettin' away and this tub of lard'll be joining those two.' His pistol jabbed at the bleeding corpses in the street. Then with focused intent, he added, 'Now stay back. And don't forget to tell yer kids it was the Red

River Gang what done this, led by Texas Jack Cantrell.' Modesty was not one of the gang leader's most endearing qualities.

Riding double with Jeffrey precariously clinging on to the pommel, Cantrell spurred his cayuse down the main street followed by the remaining three riders. Yipping and hallooing, they fired their pistols into the buildings on either side to keep the citizenry from offering any further resistance.

Two miles clear of the town limits, the quaking bank manager was unceremoniously dumped on his rear end. Raucous cat calls echoed in his ear as the confined tension rapidly drained away and the gang disappeared from view in a plume of choking white dust.

5

Sebastian Kyte

A stiff wind had blown up from the south. It was strong enough to whip the dry arid sand of the Sacramento Plains into a spiralling opaque haze that blotted all landmarks from view. Largo pulled down his hat, squinting from between narrowed eyes. A red necker covering nose and mouth attempted to contain the stinging grains of sand.

These desert storms could blow themselves out in a matter of minutes, or pummel the landscape non-stop for a week. If it lasted more than an hour, Largo knew he would have to sit this one out to the bitter end. Not a gratifying prospect as he wanted to get back to Alamogordo quickly to secure that reward money. With Billy the Kid now headed across the Del Macho Sink to Fort Sumner carrying a new bounty of a thousand bucks, he was keen to get on his tail.

He struck the pommel with his gloved fist in exasperation. The steady trot across the rolling plateau-land had slowed to barely more than a plod.

'Why now, damn you?' he yelled impotently at the seething ferment. The angry retort was instantly snatched away by the howling blast.

Normally cool and detached from any visible show of irritation, the bounty-hunter felt distinctly frustrated. He had missed the Kid by a mere couple of hours. And there was no point in following. The Sink was a bad place, notorious for its endless splay of box canyons and dried-up arroyos. He could wander for days, even weeks amidst the jagged rocks and pinnacles losing himself like many had done before, their bones picked clean by scavenging vultures and left to bleach in the hot sun. Such was the folly of man's arrogant disregard for this savage land.

Largo had more sense.

His best bet would be to head east for the Pecos and then follow the river north to Fort Sumner. But it was the long way round, and this damn blasted storm didn't help none. Some other gunsel could beat him to it.

He tweaked Dancer's flattened ears, patting her flank to encourage the tired horse. The response was a muted whinny after which the horse trudged onward, head bowed but undeterred. Nothing like a sand storm for sapping a mount's energy, mused the rider. All they could do was see it through.

Dancer stumbled as a pair of jack-rabbits scuttled between her legs searching out their own refuge. Somewhere amidst the heaving turmoil, a vulture cawed to its mate. The storm's demented ululation seemed to be intensifying. A surging blast whistled tunelessly through the fractured skeins of rock bordering the trail to produce its own ghoulish melody. And so it continued, unrelenting, for what appeared like a lifetime. In effect it was little more than two hours.

Then he saw it.

A fleeting glimpse of blue through the eddying curtain of grit. There it was again, to his left. This time more pronounced, clearer, revealing the world beyond. And as suddenly as it had erupted, the storm passed onward, scurrying up the trail leaving man and beast covered in a thick yellow coating.

Largo gave silent thanks to the Man upstairs. He stepped down, slapping the thick layer of sand from the two of them with his hat. Then, uncorking a water bottle, he tipped a generous measure into his hat.

'You first, gal. A man can allus wait.'

Dancer slurped gratefully. Sand storms were known for sucking the last drop of moisture from every living thing in their path.

It was early afternoon when Largo gratefully drew to a halt outside the marshal's office in Alamagordo. Without waiting for a formal invitation, he barged straight into the small room.

'That reward money arrived yet?' he demanded, without any formality.

Taken aback for an instant, Ramage grabbed for his gun. A scowling glare of recognition found him slumping back into his seat.

'Feller could get hisself plugged blundering in here like that,' he hissed tartly, wincing at the sudden jarring to his injured shoulder.

'Answer the question, will yuh?'

Ramage smirked. 'In some kinda hurry then?' he quipped lightly, enjoying the other's irritation.

Largo's eyes hardened, fastening onto the lawman. But he didn't rise to the bait. Then he noticed that Ramage was wearing a sling. For a minute the money was forgotten.

He pointed to the injured arm.

'What happened to you then?' A throaty chortle was followed by, 'All that dough too heavy for yuh?'

Ramage gritted his teeth as he fished into a drawer with his free hand.

'Here's yer blood money,' he snapped, curtly throwing the bundle onto the desk. 'And I hope it chokes yuh!'

The vehemence in the marshal's blunt riposte brought a frown to Largo's puckered brow.

'Easy there, Marshal. No need to get all riled up,' he averred, picking up the wad and flicking through the heap of bills. Satisfied, he stuck them into the inside pocket of his jacket. 'I was only joshin'.'

Ramage scrambled to his feet, a dark cast enveloping his hard features.

'It ain't no damn joke havin' the bank robbed,' he snapped. Then, prodding at his shoulder, added a terse rejoinder, 'And this here is a knife wound courtesy of one of them danged killers.'

'Killers yuh say?' said Largo, showing interest as well as concern.

'Young teller by the name of Jane Challener.' Ramage lowered his head, the broad shoulders sagging. It was clear that he blamed himself for allowing such a thing to happen on his patch. Shaking his head, he splashed a hefty slug of whiskey into a glass, tipping the contents down his throat. Any anger that had threatened to overflow dissolved. A pallid cast elbowed away the normal ruddiness. The marshal was almost in shock.

'When did this happen?' Largo recognized the symptoms, sympathized even.

'Day you left for Lincoln,' came back the flat response.

'Four days back!' The bounty-hunter let out a low whistle. Then his mouth tightened, the rugged contours rippling as the opportunity for new business raised its head. A steely glint crept into his eye.

'Any bounty been offered on this gang yet?' he asked, trying to inject a casual nonchalance into the enquiry.

Ramage looked at him askance. Then uttered a manic howl of laughter. He slapped the desk with his free hand in glee. A crazed leer contorted his features.

Largo's brow furrowed in a quizzical frown.

'You bet your boots there's a bounty,' roared the marshal. He was clearly relishing something. 'Jeffreys, the bank manager, has been given the go ahead from his head office in Santa Fe to offer five grand — dead or alive!'

Largo shook his head in bewilderment.

'Five big ones?'

'You betcha,' crowed Ramage leaping to his feet, 'And you know what, mister?'

'I'm sure yer gonna tell me.'

The marshal couldn't wait to get it out.

'You're too damn late. Too late, d'yuh hear?'

'What in tarnation are you on about?' rasped Largo, his patience with this crazy galoot quickly evaporating.

'Feller came in day before yesterday. Said he'd take on the job.' Ramage's lips drew back in a wild smirk revealing teeth heavily yellowed with too much baccy chewing. 'So Jeffreys took him on. No questions asked. Signed him up to bring in the entire gang.'

Reaching across the desk, Largo seized the whiskey bottle and took a hefty gulp. Then he gave the marshal a look of measured intent.

'This jasper got a handle?' he asked, imbibing another slug.

'Real snappy gopher by the name of Kyte. Sebastian Kyte.'

Halfway to Largo's open maw for a third time, the bottle stopped. His whole body tensed.

Ramage immediately read the signs. 'You know this dude?'

For a full minute Largo remained stationary, still as a tailor's dummy. Then he slowly nodded, his glassy eyes peering into an indeterminate distance. 'You could say we're acquainted.' The bottle of whiskey resumed its short journey. 'But only by reputation.'

Now the marshal was all ears.

Two professional gunfighters in a town the size of Alamagordo was big news. How would they react to each other? Would a showdown be the likely result? And which one would come out of it still on his feet? Chet Ramage was no coward, nor was he a fool. A small-town marshal used to squaring petty quarrels and minor felonies, he felt out of his depth following the bank robbery. Maybe it was best just to let the pair get on with it. Then he could tidy up after them.

'Where is he stayin'?'

Largo's question broke into the marshal's anxious cogitations.

'Taken a room over at the Imperial Hotel,' replied Ramage. 'You aimin' to pay this jigger a visit? 'Cos I don't want no trouble.'

'You already got it,' retorted Largo hustling out of the door.

Ramage shuffled round his desk and hurried over to the window. The bounty-hunter was already making a beeline for the hotel on the opposite side of the street.

News travels fast in a small town.

And all eyes were fastened on the tall gunfighter as he purposefully crossed the street. People stopped what they were doing, and watched, expectant. Even the dogs were interested. A dirty bone being scrapped over was forgotten. The lowing breeze died away to leave animated tumbleweeds marooned beneath wagons.

Largo pushed open the door and entered the garish interior of the town's only decent hotel. Velvet window drapes matched the burgundy decor of the heavy flock wallpaper, not to mention the cloying scent of cheap perfume.

Behind the reception counter lounged a small dude with slicked down black hair and a long nose. But it was the big ears sticking out like flags that reminded Largo of a surly rodent. As he approached, the polecat suddenly broke out of his lethargic pose.

'Can I help you, sir?' he asked, in a high-pitched croak, almost a squeak. Largo smiled to himself, but his hard features remained inscrutable, brusque and businesslike.

'You have a man by the name of Kyte staying here.'

It was a statement of fact, rather than a question.

'Mr Kyte is out visiting the bank at the moment,' said the desk clerk, his pointed nose twitching nervously. 'Can I take a message?'

'Mr Kyte is leaving,' retorted Largo ignoring the little man's request. 'Have his things brought down.'

'I haven't been told anything about this,' puffed the clerk, trying to inject some authority into the situation. 'The gentleman is booked in until the end of the week.'

'He's changed his mind,' rapped Largo, with a brittle inflection, 'And I'm tellin' yuh to pack his bags.' The Colt revolver leapt into his hand, the blue snout pointed unerringly at the stunned clerk. 'Unless of course you wanna argue the point with my friend here?'

'N-no, of c-course not, sir. I'll

arrange it immediately.'

'You do that.' Largo encouraged the stuttering polecat with a brisk jab in the stomach. The fellow rushed up the stairs in a blind panic. A minute later he was back toting a large carpet-bag which he placed in the middle of the lobby as indicated by Largo.

The bounty-hunter offered him a wickedly unctuous smile. 'Now we wait,' he said, sitting down to one side.

It was another half-hour before the hotel door opened and a tall, well-dressed man entered. He stopped inside the door, legs apart.

Clad in a dark-blue suit, crisp white shirt and necktie, Largo noticed that he was much older than he had surmised — at least fifty, with stray wisps of iron-grey hair trailing from beneath a wide-brimmed navy hat. Square jawed and ruggedly handsome, it was obvious that Kyte had never been short of female admirers. A neatly trimmed goatee beard streaked with silver and topped by a waxed moustache gave him the appearance of a tenderfoot — a man easily duped by more nefarious denizens inhabiting frontier townships.

Adopting the easy-going, somewhat naive manner of the greenhorn came easily to Sebastian Kyte. And it gave him an edge, an advantage that the watchful younger man was quick to appreciate.

To Largo's trained eye, the hand resting easily on the polished rosewood butt of a Smith & Wesson .45 Schofield was no idle manoeuvre. Balanced by its twin on the opposite hip, it was clear that here was a man who knew which end did the killing. Rumour had it that Kyte had become a dual *pistolero* to accommodate the fifteen plus notches he was reckoned to have earned.

Soulful eyes of the deepest mahogany surveyed the lobby from beneath thick brows. They said nothing yet spoke volumes, instantly recording the bizarre scenario that was unfolding.

A lone finger tapped the gun butt. The steady beat dutifully matched the ticking rhythm of the wall clock. Nobody spoke. A tense atmosphere hung heavy in the air.

Largo was impressed. So this was the legendary Colonel Sebastian Kyte. A hero of the Southern cause, decorated for bravery by Robert E. Lee himself, he had somehow chosen, or been pushed, along the wrong trail to gloryland.

On the surface, Largo appeared calm, unruffled, but inside his guts were churning. It was a long time since that had happened. This guy was no ordinary gun-toter, of that he was certain. Kyte was one of the few gunfighters who had perfected the cross-draw of two guns simultaneously.

Largo knew his own worth with a single shooter, but two! It was a strange feeling, unnerving. As if the guy knew the score and was playing him like a trout on a fishing line.

He shrugged off the notion. It was time for the showdown.

Behind the counter, the hotel clerk

likewise sensed the impending confrontation. And, like a rabbit faced by a snake, he was totally mesmerized — unable to move, frightened that any sudden shift might precipitate terminal gunplay.

Largo waited. It was Kyte's move.

A rolling southern drawl broke the taut silence. It was addressed to the clerk.

'Why is my bag down here in the lobby?' The delivery was slow, a laconic query edged with a hint of steel. 'I booked in for a week.'

The clerk opened his mouth. It flapped uselessly like a stranded trout.

'I asked you a question, mister.' An icy glower bored deep into the quaking man.

'This g-gentleman s-said you were ch-checking out, Mr Kyte sir.' The words jerked out in a staccato fusillade of pure terror.

Kyte's rigid gaze intensified. Deliberately, he ignored Largo who was still sitting in the corner.

'I gave no such instruction. Return the bag to my room.'

'Y-yes, sir.' The clerk gingerly emerged from behind the comforting protection of the counter. Bending to pick up the carpet bag, he felt completely exposed.

The sound of a scraping chair drifted from the corner as Largo stood up and moved into the orbit of yellow light cast by a wall lamp.

'The gentleman's leavin',' he said, resting a hand on his own revolver.

Kyte slowly swung to face him as the clerk hovered, torn between two opposing forces.

'Take the bag upstairs,' repeated Kyte evenly.

'He's leavin'.'

That was when the poor sap threw up his arms, uttered a frantic howl of anguish and dashed from the hotel lobby into the street.

'It appears that we have what our southern neighbours term a Mexican stand-off,' said Kyte, holding the younger man with a steady yet unflinching regard.

Largo met the gaze full on.

'I was here first,' he stated firmly. 'Took out Hambone Walker for the poke. Then headed north for a few days until the reward money was delivered from Roswell.' A tight grimace cracked the flinty visage challenging the other man.

'Hambone Walker.' Kyte nodded, offering his adversary a mark of respect. 'That's one tough hombre. Been after him myself for weeks.'

'Well, you were too late,' smirked Largo.

'Just like you, my friend.' Kyte's ribbed contours wrinkled into a smile. Then he continued in a blasé mien. 'Don't make no difference anyway.'

Largo afforded him a quizzical frown. 'How d'yuh figure that?' he quipped uneasily.

'I've been given the official go-ahead from the bank. All legal and above board. And I got it all down in writing.'

'Mind if I see this official document?'

'Not at all.' The man in blue slipped

a hand into his inside pocket. The move sparked an overt tension in Largo's tough hide. Kyte smiled as he slowed the move carefully extracting the sealed envelope. 'Signed by the bank president himself.'

He passed it to Largo who stepped back a pace seemingly to give it his undivided attention. Apparently satisfied, he then withdrew a cigar stub from his vest pocket and lit up. Holding the other man's interested gaze, he applied the flickering vesta to a corner of the all-important document. The flame instantly took hold, quickly devouring the thick paper. Largo let the remnants drop to the floor then ground them into dust with his boot heel.

A slow smile played across the craggy face. He said nothing, awaiting the reaction that failed to materialize. Instead, the older man took out a briar pipe, lit up by striking a lucifer on Largo's stubbly chin. Applying the lighted match to the bowl, he sucked hard, still maintaining that stoic appraisal.

Satisfied that the pipe was fired up to his satisfaction, Kyte puffed a stream of smoke into Largo's face.

The young man held his breath, eyes watering. With a supreme effort, he kept a tight grip on himself. His whole being cried out to slam a knuckled fist into this hard-assed old man.

The altercation, challenging yet unobtrusive, had attracted a few onlookers. Men sensed the sudden chill in the atmosphere. A wagon drew to a halt in the middle of the street. A cowpuncher emerging from the Painted Lady came to a sudden halt. Soon the two gunfighters had an audience peering through the open door of the hotel. All were interested spectators, eager for some action that did not involve them.

It was Kyte who finally broke the taut silence. His voice was low, little more than a whisper. The onlookers strained their ears. 'You figure that was the only copy?' He didn't wait for a reply. 'Surely you don't take me for such a naive tenderfoot. There's plenty more where that came from, I can assure you. And the original is locked up, safe and sound, well away from loose cannons . . . and surly young tinhorns.'

That's when Largo moved. But Kyte had read his thoughts. In the bite of a rattler's fang, one of the Schofields leapt from its holster jabbing into Largo's belly.

The onlookers tensed, expectant, eyes bulging in eager anticipation.

Time stood still in the Imperial Hotel.

Then Kyte's gnarled features relaxed. The taciturn appraisal softened, though he was sufficiently astute to maintain control of the situation. The revolver's barrel never wavered.

'We don't have to be on opposing sides, you and me,' he said, extracting a silver cigar case from his inside pocket and offering it to Largo. The younger man eyed the open case suspiciously, but his flinty glare eased down as the tension between the two men moderated. He accepted the cigar whilst Kyte applied a match, at the same time holstering his pistol.

'What you got in mind?' asked Largo, drawing smoke deep into his lungs.

'Let's you and me talk this through over a drink,' responded Kyte turning away. 'The Imperial also does a mighty fine steak.' He chuckled at the other man's puzzled expression. 'On me, of course.'

Largo's shoulders lifted in a casual shrug as he followed the older man into the hotel restaurant.

Disappointed at the lacklustre outcome, the crowd soon dispersed.

6

Making Plans

Following one of the finest meals he had enjoyed in a good while, all courtesy of the flamboyant yet enigmatic Sebastian Kyte, Largo had sunk his third coffee and was lighting up a large Havana. The ageing gunfighter had waxed eloquently about his adventures during the war as a colonel in charge of munitions fighting for the South.

After being discharged, he had surreptitiously commandeered more than his fair share of weaponry in a bid to root out the skunks who had murdered his parents and burnt down the family home.

'Evil bastards with no allegiance to anything except lining their own pockets,' he stressed with vehemence. 'North or South. It didn't matter a hoot to scum like that.' It had taken him six months. But eventually, through persistence and tenacity, he had run them to ground. By then, there was a substantial bounty on their heads.

'I gave them more of a chance than they ever gave Ma and Pa,' he opined, the brown eyes misting over at the painful recollection. 'There were only two of the original five left. The others had been shot down during other robberies.' A smile broke the stiff demeanour. 'Still, that amounted to three thousand dollars. From then on, I was hooked.'

Largo eyed him coolly.

'So how come you're prepared to split the reward?'

He posed the question that had been bothering him all through the meal. All bounty men worked alone. Sharing the loot with others was outside their *modus operandi*. Trust was the main priority. Largo trusted no one. Only on one occasion had he ever thrown in with another jasper, and Jimmy Ringo was now pushing up the yucca in Durango for trying to backshoot him.

Then another thought struck home. 'Why have you come to Alamagordo in the first place? You said yerself that it was a surprise to have stumbled on Hambone Walker.'

For a full minute Kyte sat still, staring into the distance, as if in a dream. When he finally spoke, the words were cracked, full of pent-up emotion.

'I want that gang,' he snarled. 'Not since my parents were killed have I wanted anything so bad.' The utterance was literally torn from his throat. His fist, tightly balled, struck down on the table. Other diners looked up, disturbed by the sudden noise. Kyte took no notice. 'Texas Jack Cantrell and his bunch are going to pay dearly for what they've done. They even boasted of it. Proud to have gunned down a young girl.'

Disgust and abhorrence gleamed in the colonel's eyes. Pure unadulterated loathing oozed from every pore of his being.

Largo was puzzled.

Why was this gang so different?

Kyte's frenzied outburst was soon quelled as he regained control of his feelings. Men in his profession couldn't afford to let personal vendettas cloud their judgement.

'So?' pressed Largo.

Kyte's eyes had shrunk to mere pinpricks, tiny chunks of coal glinting in the beams of light slanting through the restaurant window.

'You're right, Mr Largo,' he stated firmly. 'My presence here is no coincidence. I came to visit with my estranged wife and daughter.' His head bowed revealing a bald patch of tanned flesh against the thinning grey hair. Suddenly he looked all of his fifty-two years, an ageing gunfighter well past his best. 'Rachel left me eight years ago. Couldn't handle the constant moving from one town to another. Can't say as I blame her. It's no life for a woman and young girl. I always intended to settle down, buy a place.' He looked up, seeking Largo's approval. 'But you know how it is. The next wanted dodger; the excitement of the chase.'

Largo nodded. He knew only too well, being caught up in the same obsession, the same dependence.

Kyte smiled, glad of a kindred spirit to whom he could unburden himself. 'She found some other guy who could offer the sort of life she wanted. Stability. A permanent home for Jane.' Again the glassy-eyed stare, the quivering lip. 'And that was that. I lost all contact until three months ago. The trail led me here.' Kyte paused to gather himself. 'Jane would have been twenty-two now.'

'Would have?'

'That's why I want you to go in with me, Largo,' said Kyte slowly and with a firm resolve. 'It was my daughter who was killed in the bank raid.'

A low whistle escaped from Largo's pursed lips.

'You can have the bounty rewards,' Kyte continued, puffing hard on his pipe. 'It's blood money to me. All I want are the bastards that shot my little girl.' His knuckles blanched white, threatening to snap the thin stem. The blood drained from his face. 'Just seeing her on that slab in the undertaker's parlour . . . ' A wave of anguish washed over the hard-bitten man hunter. Tears dribbled down his leathery cheeks.

Largo looked away. It was embarrassing to witness a grown man in such pain. What could he say? What could anyone say to a man whose only daughter has been savagely gunned down? He shuffled his feet uncomfortably.

The Good Book preached forgiveness, turning the other cheek. That was no answer for a man like Sebastian Kyte. He favoured another religious maxim — an eye for an eye! And Largo was more than willing to help him achieve that desired end.

Especially when the financial rewards

had suddenly increased immeasurably.

He stood up to leave. There were questions that needed answering, but this wasn't the time. Better to give the guy some room, a period to reflect on the future, and the past. As for the present, he was in purgatory. A personal hell that only he could deal with.

'Give me an hour,' croaked the older man struggling to regain his dignity. 'Then come up to my room and we'll figure out what's to be done.'

Largo grunted, set his hat straight and left. He felt the need of a something stronger than coffee. The more comforting attractions of the Longhorn Saloon beckoned invitingly.

Outside, a stiff wind had blown up. Tumbleweed scuttled along the street anxious to beat the impending storm. Rusty signboards creaked. A crackle of forked lightning split the ether as dark clouds trundled across the sky obliterating the sun's harsh glare. Growling with animosity, they appeared to sense and commiserate with the old gunfighter's trauma. As if in response to some predestined orchestration, an angry drumming started up on the wooden overhang. It sounded like an army on the march.

An army of two in search of vengeance and bounty!

'You still around?' Wrapped up in some serious ruminations, Largo hadn't noticed the marshal's approach. 'Figured you'd have hit the trail by now, there bein' no easy pickings in this town any more.'

Largo regarded the lawman with a baleful grimace, the grey eyes coolly amused. No comment passed his lips.

Ramage pressed home his supposed advantage. 'Kyte given you the brush-off then?' The moustache flickered with ill-disguised conceit.

'Maybe,' came back the rather too blasé rejoinder as he pushed past the marshal. 'Then again,' — he winked conspiratorially — 'maybe not.'

Ramage was left to scratch his head, unsure what to believe.

★ ★ ★

Just as the hall clock behind the Imperial reception counter was striking three bells, Largo rapped on the door of number five at the end of the first-floor corridor. Clutched in his hand was a bottle of the best Kentucky bourbon.

'Enter,' came the brisk response.

Kyte was leaning against the window frame staring out at the lowering sky. A grim expression clouded his distinguished features. He gave a sigh, as if empathizing with the dour prospect on the far side of the glass. Then, swinging briskly on his heel, he motioned for Largo to take a seat. No longer the slack-jawed old soldier of the previous hour, Kyte was once again the business-like practitioner of man-hunting.

Largo poured them both a drink.

'So, Mr Largo,' began the older man raising his glass, 'are you with me?'

The young gunfighter hesitated. He was not yet convinced. When he eventually spoke, it was with a slow but even drawl. 'You seem to be hell bent on catchin' up with these critters,' he said, 'and I can sympathize with your reasons.' The grey eyes hardened. 'But it seems to me as if it's your heart that's runnin' the show. In my experience, when a man lets his feelings overrule his head, there's big trouble a-brewin' up, and I want no part of that.'

'I hear you, young man. And I agree wholeheartedly.' Kyte took a long pull at the bourbon, savouring the dry cut as it simmered down his throat. 'You saw me at my worst an hour past. That man has been consigned to the back burner. From now on, we run this on strictly practical terms. No hysterics, no displays of sentiment.' Again he raised his glass. 'That suit you?'

This time, Largo clinked.

'Just one thing,' he said.

'Name it.'

'With you havin' the job all official like, signed, sealed and delivered in your name — '

Kyte interrupted with a coarse guffaw.

'You figure I'll run out on you once the job's done? Is that it?'

'It's happened before.'

A wistful smile floated across Kyte's ribbed features.

Then he suggested, 'What if we were to mosey on down to the bank right now and I were to destroy the original contract? Would that satisfy your suspicious nature?'

'Sounds OK by me,' replied Largo.

'But you have to give me your solemn promise to see this darned business through,' stressed Kyte thrusting out his bearded chin. Pausing he added, 'To its bitter finale.'

Just then, the sound of gunfire rattled the window frame. It came from the street outside. Both men tensed, their hands automatically dropping to the ever-present hardware. The riotous fusillade was immediately followed by a flurry of ribald laughter. Just a few cowpunchers letting off steam.

Kyte smiled, levelling a cool regard on his new partner. Which one of them had been faster on the draw? A like question passed through Largo's mind. Perhaps neither of them would ever find out. He fervently hoped so.

After holstering their revolvers, Kyte held out his hand.

'Partners?'

The grip was firm, solid and enduring.

'Partners,' replied Largo categorically. Again they clinked glasses. Then Largo said, 'This gang has been causin' a ruckus all over the territory for more'n two years. And nobody's gotten near to 'em so far. They just seem to disappear into thin air after each job.' Then he voiced his main concern. 'How are we gonna catch up with them where everyone else has failed?'

Kyte speared him with a shrewd look, pulling hard on his pipe before replying.

'That isn't strictly true,' he averred slowly.

Largo frowned.

The older man went on to outline his

encounter with the Red River bunch. By chance he had been making a deposit in the South Central Bank at Socorro at the very same moment that the gang had chosen to rob it. Like the other customers, he had been forced to drop his weapons and lie on the floor.

'Most embarrassing for a man in my profession,' he grumbled, shaking his head, 'being forced to chew dirt while a bunch of hard-nosed villains come a-calling.'

Largo couldn't restrain a brittle guffaw. 'That musta bin some sight.'

'It's no joke, I can tell you,' grumbled Kyte defensively. 'Cantrell even took a shine to the gold watch and chain that was presented to me personally by President Jefferson Davis.' His eyes misted over.

'So what happened?' pressed Largo, caught up with other man's vibrant narration.

Quickly regaining his composure, he hurried on with a wry glint in his eye. 'Well, mister, them jiggers hadn't reckoned with Sebastian Kyte. No sirree. Soon as they done the business inside the bank and skedaddled, I was out of there and priming up the Spencer. It's fitted with a specially extended barrel for long range accuracy. Them there fellows were almost out of town thinking they had escaped without so much as a scratch, doubtless yipping and heehawing to each other about how easy it had been. Then . . . ' Kyte made as if to fire the rifle. 'Bang! Only took but a single shot, and one of them jaspers was eating dust.'

'Much as I've enjoyed listenin' to your adventures, Colonel,' butted in Largo, 'I can't figure how it helps us now.'

'Patience, my dear fellow, patience,' chided Kyte in remonstration. 'You young rannigans are all the same. Too darned impulsive. Just ease down and all will be revealed.' Kyte filled up their empty glasses. 'Dogface Mendoza was the guy who was shot, only a scratch as it happens. My aim was a bit off due to

the distressing circumstances, you understand.'

'Just get to the point,' growled Largo.

'This morning I received a wire from
a contact in Socorro informing me that
Mendoza is being transferred to Fort
Summer to stand trial. And that's
where you come in.'

'Me?'

Kyte nodded earnestly.

'You're going to rescue him and offer
your services to the gang. I can't do it
because they know my face. But they've
never seen you, have they?'

Largo shook his head, his mouth
gaping wide. He was completely non-
plussed.

Kyte continued undeterred. 'Rescu-
ing a *bandido* of Mendoza's calibre will
get you into the gang's secret hideout.
Allow you to gain their trust.'

'And where will you be while all this
is a-goin' on?'

'Don't worry. I'll be keeping an eye
on things. Trailing you. At a distance, of
course. Then once you've been accepted

by Cantrell and his boys, we can make plans to net them all in one fell swoop.' Kyte stared hard at his partner. 'So what d'you say?'

Largo remained silent. Pushing back his chair, he stood up and walked over to the window and lit up a fresh cigar. Idly he picked at a sliver of rotten wood. Thinking.

Following due deliberation, and having chewed over the ramifications of Kyte's plan, he turned to face his partner.

'Got it all figured out, ain't yuh?' he drawled. 'I do all the dirty work, riskin' life and limb. Then you come bustin' in at the finish to claim all the glory.'

Kyte carefully set his glass down and drew himself up to his full height of six three. Hard flakes of steel glittered in his staring orbs.

'Just you remember it was my daughter that was killed. And it's you who will be receiving the full reward when this job is completed.'

Largo's tanned features coloured.

'Clean forgot that, didn't you, partner?'

'Erm!' muttered Largo, disconcerted.

'So you should have no complaints about taking on a few extra risks and letting an old jasper like me act as backup. Are we agreed?'

Largo hummed and hawed under his breath, then mumbled out of the corner of his mouth, 'OK, it's agreed.' Finishing with a stiff retort, 'But make danged certain you have my back covered, y'hear?'

'Now that's settled,' said Kyte lightening his tone with a wry smile, 'we'd better hit the trail.'

'What's the hurry?'

'Mendoza is being moved from Socorro at dawn tomorrow by the sheriff. All on his lonesome,' replied Kyte, already gathering his meagre belongings together.

'You sure as hell are well informed,' broke in Largo, clearly in awe of his new sidekick.

'As luck would have it, my ex-wife's brother runs a store in Socorro.' He uttered a sardonic chuckle. 'And you know how them fellers make it their business to know everything.' Adopting a more serious vein, he continued, 'I think you ought to make your move after dark. If we leave within the hour, by my reckoning you should cut their trail at Willard Pass.'

'Don't leave much time fer sayin' our goodbyes.'

Kyte shrugged his broad shoulders.

'I am sure that Marshal Ramage will be more than happy to see our trail dust.'

Largo joined him in a genial spate of laughter at the notion.

'Yuh ain't wrong there, Seb,' he chortled.

The familiarity came easy. He liked this man, and was beginning to have a close affinity with the ageing gun-fighter, something he had always shied away from in the past. Yet Sebastian Kyte imbued an aura of trust. The guy was nothing if not sincere. There was no deceit about him, no false imagery. Largo had an innate feeling that the guy would back him up all the way. Right down to the wire.

7

Pursuit

'Shake yer ass, greaser!'

Sheriff Corby Lanning rattled a tin plate across the cell bars. The first shot of pale yellow had broken through the tiny window set high in the adobe walls heralding the false dawn. It would be sun-up in half an hour and Lanning wanted to be on the trail to Fort Sumner by then. He knew the trip would take the best part of three days. And with a slippery galoot like Dogface Mendoza in tow, the quicker he completed the handover to the court authorities the better.

Mendoza grunted in his sleep. Again the jangly scraping on the bars. No response other than a broken snort. The sheriff sniggered to himself as he returned to the outer office. Picking up a tin mug, he threw the coffee dregs into a waste bucket and dipped the mug into a water butt. Then he went back to the single cell behind him.

'You asked for it,' he muttered to himself with a sour grin, flinging the contents at the recumbent form on the cell bunk.

'Aaaaaagh!' The discordant roar elicited a harsh laugh from Lanning. But the dousing had achieved its aim. Mendoza was instantly wide awake. He shook himself like a disturbed hound. '*Madre de dios.* Why you do thees thing, *hombre*?' he snarled in a lilting mix of Spanish and pidgin English.

'Rise and shine, Dogface,' rapped the sheriff brightly. 'Time we was a-takin' you to visit the hangman.'

Mendoza growled, his thin lips parting in a warped snarl. 'You no be a-calling me Dogface. My name is Juan Castillo de Mendoza.'

'You look like a snub-nosed bull terrier to me . . . Dogface.' Then a dark cast clouded the lawman's craggy features. 'And I intend to be sittin' right there on the front row when they hang yuh. Seein' as how it was my brother that you gunned down in the street.' An ugly snarl crinkled the sheriff's handsome features. 'Yuh dog-faced bastard.'

Mendoza held himself in check. He could see pure poison in the venomous look and could smell the hate emanating from the law man.

Dogface! He hated the name. It had been acquired following a drunken fracas when his already broad proboscis was squashed flat to his face, the bone broken in three places. The injury had never set properly leaving the once handsome Mexican with a nickname that had since been the cause of three killings.

Thereafter, he had been forced to flee his father's grandiose hacienda and take to the owlhoot trail. But the ostentatious arrogance of his aristocratic upbringing had never deserted him. Even in the company of raw-boned *bandidos* like the Red River Gang, he

106

displayed an aloof disdain for his less well-bred *compadres*.

It showed in the extravagant clothes he always wore. Silver spurs, fancy duds, not to mention the tooled leather saddle. But the Mexican was no chicken-livered skunk, as those who had chided him about his nickname had discovered to their cost. And Lanning was only too well aware that the greaser would skewer his guts to a tree trunk at the first opportunity.

He ordered Mendoza to stand back from the cell door as he unlocked it.

'Now turn around so that I don't have to look at that ugly mug of yourn,' he growled. A surly frown concentrated the ribbed contours of Mendoza's swarthy face, but he complied nonetheless.

'Hands behind your back,' ordered Lanning.

'You no trust me, *señor*?'

'Like I would an angry sidewinder,' replied the sheriff, as he snapped a pair of steel cuffs on the proffered wrists.

Out of his pocket he withdrew a hunk of cheese and some sourdough biscuits. 'Time for breakfast,' he announced, throwing the food onto the dirt floor. Quickly backing out, he slammed the cell door shut.

Mendoza looked at the unsavoury offering through slitted eyes, his mouth curling in disgust. 'How I supposed to eat that?' he asked.

Lanning chuckled gleefully. 'You're the mangy hound. Now act like one.'

A crazed howl of rage erupted from the Mexican's open maw. His scowling face turned a vivid puce. Cursing volubly, he poured scorn on Lanning's parentage. All to no avail. The sheriff merely guffawed even louder. Then he left with a final retort, 'Eat up, Dogface. Gotta keep your strength up fer the hangman.'

Within the hour they had hit the trail heading due east towards the distant Gallinas Peak. A low breeze rippled the trees, tugging at the brim of Lanning's brown stetson. Already, the sun was making its presence felt, smothering the arid terrain in a golden glow. Indeterminate landscape features slowly sharpened into focus as the light strengthened.

The sheriff led the way, his prisoner securely pinioned to the saddle by his feet as well as his hands. There was no way Lanning was about to give the wily Mexican any opportunity to jump him. Justice for his brother would be done according to the due process of the law. And he would enjoy every minute of it.

★ ★ ★

Largo and Kyte had been in the saddle all night. Progress had been slow due to a dense mantle of cloud obscuring the sky for much of the time. Thankfully, the rain had stopped. Only when the moon's ethereal radiance had broken through were they able to spur to more than a canter. At such times the silvery flush gave the landscape a monochrome appearance in which bizarre apparitions leapt out at them from the shadows in the guise of mythical fiends from another dimension.

Had the unlikely duo been of a nervous disposition, the macabre journey could have had dire consequences. As it was, both were pragmatists, men with a mission that no flights of fancy were about to dislodge.

Largo actually relished night riding. It was he who took the lead allowing Dancer to pick her own course amidst the myriad of rocky defiles and gorges that split the terrain north east of Alamagordo. Maintaining that direction was all that was required for them to eventually cut the trail of Sheriff Lanning and his prisoner. Thankfully, Colonel Kyte was able to make use of his prismatic compass in achieving that end.

Nevertheless, morning came as a relief from the strain of constantly being on the alert.

By mid-afternoon, they had reached Coyote Springs, a trading post that was little more than a log cabin stuck in the middle of a vast wasteland of sagebrush and mesquite. Three horses were grazing in the corral to one side. A plume of white smoke snaking from the stove-pipe chimney was whipped away by the stiff wind. But at least it informed the two riders that the place was occupied.

Being the only source of water in the region midway between Socorro and Fort Sumner made it an ideal stopping off point for travellers. Their quarry would have to stop here to replenish their canteens. If they hadn't already done so.

Largo stuck his ear to the heavy plank door. The muted hum of voices told him there were at least three rannigans on the far side. Pushing open the door, both men stood to one side so as not to present an easy target to any nervous trigger fingers that might be in residence.

The voices stilled. But nothing happened.

Then a gruff rasp broke the tense atmosphere.

'Come along in, gents. No tin stars hidin' round the corner.' The speaker chuckled at his witty retort.

Then another voice piped up. 'Turkey Jim Dooley is known in these parts for keeping a friendly and open house.'

Largo cautiously peered round the corner, his revolver leading the way.

'No need fer any shootin' irons,' chided an old jasper who was busy polishing a glass with a grubby towel. He was sporting heavy florid jowls covered by a bushy grey beard. 'First drink is allus on the house.'

It was obvious how the proprietor had come by his name. Largo smiled replacing his gun in its holster. The guy's guttural tones even sounded like a gobbler. Dooley was lounging behind the makeshift bar which comprised nothing more than two planks supported by a barrel at each end.

Turkey Jim looked from one to the other expectantly. The hooded eyes danced and flickered but had a cold flinty cast. 'So what kin I be doin' fer you gents?' he asked, trying to inject some measure of welcome into the tired vocals.

It was Kyte who spoke.

'All we want is some information.' His tone was even but had a gritty edge. He held Dooley with a menacing regard.

The old guy shook his head, running a set of grubby fingers through the greasy mat of thinning sandy hair. 'Don't know about that,' he trilled, tipping rotgut whiskey into a couple of glasses. 'Information is a mighty expensive commodity round here. That's if'n I got the answers.'

Kyte picked up the glass and took a sip.

'If it's any worse than this hooch, then it ain't worth a bent nickel.'

'There's no call fer that kind of talk, mister,' bleated Dooley, backing away from the counter, his hand straying towards a shelf behind him. 'No man oughta grumble about a free drink.'

'Keep them hands on the counter if you wanna see the day out.' Largo's voice was coolly menacing, his sixgun pointing unerringly at the trader's leery visage.

In the corner, two down-at-heel range bums ceased their card game watching the events unfolding before them, their gaze watchful and jittery.

Meanwhile Kyte had extracted a hefty bundle of greenbacks from his jacket. Slowly he peeled off a few and wafted them in front of Dooley's staring orbs. The old jasper was mesmerized. His mouth hung wide, saliva dribbling out the corner.

A look of greedy anticipation passed between the two drifters.

'Now,' hissed Kyte, 'about that information.'

Dooley quickly counted the notes. His nose wrinkled. The gaping eyes narrowed.

'Ten bucks, is that all?' he scoffed, 'Yuh ain't gettin' much fer that.'

But Kyte was through playing games. One second he was leaning on the bar, idly toying with his glass, the next he had Turkey Jim's scrawny neck in a vice-like grip.

Largo's gun hand swung to face the other two occupants of the room who had pushed back their chairs, hands already plucking at their own hardware. The Frontier bucked twice, its roar deafening in the enclosed space. One man spun in a tight circle clutching at his shattered collar bone. Not quite as handy with a gun, his partner was more fortunate. He quickly dropped the weapon and raised his hands.

'Don't shoot, mister,' he pleaded desperately anxious to avoid the other rannie's fate. 'I ain't gonna draw on yer.'

'Throw them hoglegs over here,' snarled Largo, emphasizing the order with his smoking pistol. 'Then see to that lump of cow dung.' He pointed to the wounded man who was rolling about on the dirt floor. 'And tell him to cut that gripin' else I'll shut him up for good.'

'Y-yessiree,' wailed the man. 'Anythin' you say.'

Satisfied that he had stymied any dissent, Largo was content to watch his partner in action.

'Now do you see what happens to jiggers who get too much above themselves, too greedy?' Kyte abruptly released the quaking trader and gently slapped the wobbling flaps of loose skin with his bowie knife. 'I'd hate for this here poker to slip.' Jerking the knife just sufficiently to draw a thin sliver of red, he continued, 'So how about that information, Mr Dooley?' It was more of a demand than a request.

'Sure, sure thing.' Dooley's voice was vibrating more than a rattler's tail as he struggled to remain absolutely still. 'Anythin' I can help you fellers with, jest ask away an' old Turkey Jim'll do his best to oblige.'

'Has Sheriff Lanning passed this way recently?'

Dooley drew in his breath before answering. 'Lanning, yuh say?'

'He's takin' a prisoner to Fort Sumner,' added Largo.

'Lanning, eh?' Dooley was stalling.

Kyte jogged his memory with a poke from the bowie. The resultant squeal was as much from the enhanced flow of crimson as the sharp jolt of pain. But it had the desired effect.

'Came through here around noon,' he stuttered casting angst-ridden looks at the two looming figures. 'Had a greaser in tow. Natty dresser fer a Mex. They was headed over to Fort Sumner — '

'We know about that,' interjected Largo, pressing fresh cartridges into the Frontier.

Kyte studied his pocket watch. It was two hours ago.

'Did he have a handle, this greaser?'

'Lanning kept callin' him Dogface.' Dooley tried to make light of it. 'Sure did have a mashed in kisser an' no mistake.'

'You ain't one to goof off about others are yuh, Turkey?' Largo shot back.

The trader snorted but advisedly kept his peace.

'Which way did they head off?' continued Kyte, releasing the panting trader. He was anxious to be away from this reeking hovel.

'Took the main trail through Willard Pass and over the Cibolas. It's a full day longer but safer. More traffic so less chance of any' — Dooley knowingly tapped his jutting snout — 'any unforeseen accidents, if yuh know what I mean.'

Largo knew only too well what he meant. He lunged at the strutting trader and hoisted him halfway across the bar top.

'You would do well not to mention that we have been askin' after this tin star and his prisoner.' He lowered his gaze and drew the thin lips back in a wicked rictus. 'If word gets out, just remember we'll be ridin' back this way.'

Then he threw the trembling fellow against the shelves behind the bar. Bottles rattled, glasses chinked and fell crashing to the floor.

The two bounty-men backed out of the door, guns cocked and threatening termination to anyone rash enough to pursue them. Mounting up, they spurred off towards the notched gap in the far mountains that was Willard Pass.

The threatening storm had passed on, pushed aside by a golden sun that burnt down from a cloudless sky. Buzzards circled ominously, floating with effortless ease on the hot thermals. Starkly etched against the deep azure backdrop, they eyed the two riders expectantly. Perhaps if they hung around long enough, their hungry wait would elicit its reward. Only the next few hours would tell.

After an hour, the two riders arrived at a break in the trail. A faded sign pointed south of east. Scrawled in red paint thereon was the legend *Fort Sumner — 85 miles*.

'This is where we part company,' announced Kyte removing his hat and dragging a bandanna across his damp brow. 'You ought to strike their camp sometime after sundown. Keep an eye open for their fire.'

'Don't you worry none, old man,' chaffed Largo taking a swig from his canteen. 'I know the score.'

'I'll take the old Indian trail to Fort Sumner. And I'll stay there until I get word from you.' Kyte held out his hand. The old soldier had also felt himself drawn inexorably closer to his younger partner. Largo could have been the son he never had.

They shook on the deal. It was a dangerous gamble that could result in Largo providing those pesky buzzards with their Sunday lunch. Kyte watched as the young manhunter cantered away across the dusty plain. A tear oozed from the corner of his eye tracking down the seamed contours and dripping unseen off the end of the solid chin. Was it for his daughter, or for

Largo? Maybe a bit of both.

Soon the tall rider disappeared behind a chaotic jumble of boulders and juniper thickets. Only then did Sebastian Kyte reset his hat straight and continue onward.

8

Rescue

As the sun slid behind a bank of cloud edging its way down below the western horizon of jagged peaks, Largo slowed his pace. Squinting his grey eyes to thin slits, the manhunter carefully scanned the shadowy terrain for a sign of his quarry. He had made good time and knew that Lanning and his prisoner could not be far ahead. But until the last glimmer of natural light had faded, he needed to be painstaking in exercising assiduous vigilance. Running across the pair too soon would spoil the plan he had worked out. Darkness had to be complete.

Dancer had thoroughly enjoyed the steady canter across the gently rolling scrubland that comprised the Gallinas Plateau. After cresting Willard Pass, the ground fell away abruptly into a deep canyon, one of many such rifts that split the Cibola Mountain fastness. From here on, far more care was required.

The grey mare was all for throwing caution to the wind and streaking headlong down the loose gradient beyond. Largo was hard pressed to keep the feisty cayuse under control. At this late stage, the last thing he wanted was to be cast afoot due to his mount suffering a sprained foreleg or worse.

Another hour passed before total darkness had enfolded the broken terrain in its tentacles. And it was a further hour before the faint glimmer of light from a camp-fire penetrated the black curtain, over to the right, and a hundred yards off the trail amidst the dense canopy of pine.

Reining to a halt, Largo gently patted Dancer's neck, leaning over and whispering softly in her perked ear.

'Now you stay calm, Dancer old gal, yuh hear? And don't be making a sound while I'm away.' He stepped down, playfully tweaking the horse's twitchy ears and blowing into her nostrils. The mount nuzzled his arm affectionately. She understood what was expected. Largo nodded. 'I know yuh won't let me down.'

One final rub and he was gone, merging into the gloomy interior of the forest.

His heart was pounding in his chest like a steam hammer; not so much from trepidation of what the coming encounter would bring, as the distinct possibility of stepping on a dry twig and giving away his presence. The last thing he wanted was a gun duel with an officer of the law where either of them might get shot. Extreme watchfulness was, therefore, needed to maintain that essential silence — a herculean task in the dark. And as the orange glow emanating from the camp-fire intensified, so Largo's nerve endings prickled remorselessly.

The chink of cutlery on tin plates informed him that a meal was being consumed. The scent of frying bacon and freshly brewed Java wafting through the enclosed canopy reminded him of his own innermost needs. Apart from chewing on a few hard tack biscuits and gnawing a stick of beef jerky, he had not eaten properly since the previous day.

He shrugged off the rumbling in his stomach. It had happened before and would doubtless occur again. The notion of eating tasty victuals flew out the window when a man hunt was under way. Thrusting the appetizing smells aside, he sank down and crawled to the edge of the clearing. In the centre, a small fire crackled and hissed. Tracers of orange flame writhed and cavorted reflecting a myriad of flies attracted by the light and the rare chance of a meal.

The lurid glow lit up the faces of the two men sitting opposite each other on either side of the fire. The sheriff, an evil and malicious grin breaking across his weathered countenance, sat resting against a saddle shovelling food into his mouth. The tin star winked in the light.

Opposite was the prisoner. It was obvious that Lanning had no intention of allowing his prisoner the slightest opportunity to jump him. Dogface Mendoza was living up to his nickname. Hands manacled behind his back with feet securely tied, he was on his knees, face down scoffing a plate of food. And Lanning was enjoying every minute of his prisoner's humiliating discomfort.

Suddenly the Mexican hauled himself upright.

Lanning stiffened, his hand reaching for the Winchester by his side.

'I need to relieve myself,' snarled Mendoza, not deigning to conceal his hate for the lawdog. 'At least untie my feet, even if you will allow me no privacy.'

'Sit back down. You ain't goin' nowhere,' Lanning snapped, resuming his meal.

'But I am bursting,' bellowed the Mexican, clearly in some distress. 'My pants, I will be fouling them.' The whining lament had a pathetic air that only served to elicit further derision from his captor.

The sheriff let out a guffaw. 'Then wet yerself, Dogface,' he cackled. 'See if I care.'

Mendoza snarled and ranted, his odious appendage flaring. Hurling abuse on the sheriff, he attempted to rush the lawman. But to no avail. It was a futile gesture as they both well knew. He slumped down, saliva dribbling from his lips, green eyes glittering with impotent rage. Lanning also sank back against his saddle, pouring a generous tot of whiskey into his coffee mug.

While this brief altercation was occurring, Largo had circled round just inside the protective layer of trees. He needed to be in position behind the sheriff. From there he could make his play.

Somewhere off to the left, a lone coyote howled at the moon, just then peeping from behind a scudding bank of cumulus. It bathed the clearing in a lustrous glow.

Largo's nerves were screwed up tight as a drum skin. His fist blanched white as he gripped the butt of the Frontier. Always the same before a showdown. And he wouldn't have it any other way. The harsh pump of adrenalin through his veins gave him an edge, that essential split second's advantage over his adversary.

Reversing the revolver so he was holding it butt forward, Largo purposefully stepped out from the shadowy recess of the trees. Once in the open, he felt exposed. It was now or never: the sheriff's back was a mere ten feet away. All it needed was a sharp clip to the side of the guy's head and he would be out of it.

But it was Mendoza's suddenly raised eyes, the greaser's taut frame that alerted the sheriff. No slouch at reading the signs, even after a few slugs of whiskey, Lanning's hand flew to the Winchester. He half turned levering the action.

A fraction too late.

Largo sprang at him. His lean body, lithe and tensile as a young puma, covered the intervening space in the flick of a gnat's wing. The gun butt glanced off the sheriff's temple.

'Aaaagh!'

A coarse rasp of pain erupted from Lanning's throat as the blow connected. But it was insufficient to lay him out cold. He slumped to one side still trying to bring the rifle to bear, an irate snarl thick with menace spewing from between pursed lips.

Largo didn't panic.

He aimed a second blow to the side of the head, hard enough to render the guy unconscious, but sufficiently controlled to prevent any permanent damage. The last thing he wanted was the blood of a dead lawdog on his hands. Once he and Mendoza had completed their disappearing act, whichever direction that entailed, he wanted to ensure the sheriff was capable of reaching civilization under his own steam.

Mendoza was now on his feet dancing around on the far side of the fire like a demented clown, tugging at the rope that secured him to a tree. Arms waving, he egged the avenging angel onward.

'Kill thee *bastardo*!' he screamed gleefully. 'Shoot heem down like thee scurvy critter he ees.'

Largo had no such intention. Leathering his gun, he slid round the fire and cut the Mexican free with his knife.

Briskly taking charge, he snapped, 'Where are your horses?'

'In the trees,' said Mendoza. Hurrying on, the Mexican enquired, 'But who are you, *compadre*, and where you come from, eh?'

'I'll tell yuh later. We ain't got no time to lose. There's a posse on my tail.' Largo didn't want to give the ex-captive any time to think. 'Saddle up and meet me back on the trail where my own cayuse is picketed.'

Then Mendoza remembered the sheriff. An ugly snarl split the once handsome facade. 'Lend me your gun, *hombre*, so I can finish off this asshole.'

Largo tenaciously nudged him towards the horses. Drawing his own weapon he cocked it stressing his rejoinder. 'You douse this fire and saddle up. I'll see to the sheriff.' Without any further preamble, he strode across the clearing and pumped three rounds at the prone figure, ensuring that they ploughed into the ground just to one side.

'That'll give the buzzards some'n to squawk about come sun up,' he shouted, injecting a measure of venom into his retort. A raucous bout of laughter followed as he kicked sand over the fire to douse the flames. 'Not to mention a welcome breakfast they never expected.' Then to Mendoza, 'Now shift yer ass. We ain't got all night.'

The brutal action, swift and decisive, appeared to satisfy the newly released outlaw who was only too relieved to have escaped a certain necktie party at Fort Sumner. A flood of ecstatic euphoria at his unexpected freedom swamped any further queries regarding the motives of his Good Samaritan. And with a supposed posse not far behind, Mendoza also was keen to split the breeze.

Soon they were spurring their mounts away from the grim campsite.

For some time they rode in silence. The cloud banks had dispersed leaving a clear sky which emphasized the bejewelled canopy overhead.

Largo took careful note from the position of the stars that they were heading east into the maze of split canyons known as the Del Macho Sink. It was the same area where he had lost touch with Billy the Kid. Maybe this was where the Red River Gang also had their hideout.

It was only later when Mendoza had simmered down, having gotten used to being a free agent once again, that he began to question his benefactor.

'What do they call you then, *amigo*?'

'The name's . . . Banner.' The slight hesitation was missed by the Mexican.

The name of Largo was well known to owlhooters throughout the western territories, if not the face. Too many of Mendoza's lawless equals had met a grisly end at his hands. Maintaining an anonymous front was essential if this plan was to have any chance of succeeding.

Mendoza looked askance at his new partner. For a second, Largo's stomach lurched.

'Ees that all?' he scoffed.

'It's enough, ain't it?'

The Mexican shrugged then adopted a pompous air as he proudly revealed his own aristocratic lineage. 'I am Juan Castillo de Mendoza and my *padre* is the largest *haciendero* in the province of Chihuahua. It would take you five days to ride from one side of his land to the other.' Mendoza was like a strutting peacock with full plumage on display. He offered his partner a condescending smile. 'But you are my *amigo*. So you call me Juan. *Si*?'

Largo could barely contain a straight

face knowing full well the origin of the snobby dude's nickname. Nevertheless, he returned the gesture with an obsequious bow.

'Now that's real charitable of you . . . Juan.' The sarcastic inflection was completely lost on the preening Mexican.

They shook hands, Largo deliberately allowing his new buddy to take the lead. The hours passed, dawn eventually drawing back the curtain of blackness. They were now well into the maze of canyons that comprised the Sink.

It was inevitable that sooner or later Mendoza would want to know why Largo had rescued him. The question came as they were cresting a rise that overlooked a deeply scoured valley, much wider and greener than anything they had so far encountered. This had to be their destination, the gang's hideout. Smoke rose from a long wooden cabin surrounded by corrals in which four mounts sauntered idly.

Mendoza reined in and eyed his partner keenly. His warped face betrayed no emotion, the animated tone level and flat when he spoke.

'Why did you rescue me then, *compadre*? It has been troubling me for the last hour.'

Largo withdrew a cigar, struck a match on his saddle horn and lit up. He drew hard, composing his thoughts. This had to be good, convincing. If he could fully win over Mendoza, then Texas Jack Cantrell and the other members of the gang would fall into line.

'After robbing the overland stage from Silver City, I figured to escape into the Cibolas. But the posse stuck to my tail like fleas on a gopher. Trouble was, the dang blasted strong box was empty. So the law was after me and I had nary a bent nickel to show for it.'

He paused drawing smoke into his lungs whilst glancing over, trying to read his partner's expression. It remained blank, inscrutable.

'I'd heard the sheriff of Socorro was hauling an important member of the Red River Gang over to Fort Sumner,' he continued. 'When I caught sight of your camp-fire, I figured it had to be you. Reckoned if I helped you out of a hole, you could maybe introduce me to the rest of the gang and let me hook up. As you saw back there, I ain't afraid to haul off with my smokepole. Another gunhand could be useful to yuh.' Another pregnant pause, another tense appraisal. 'So, what d'yuh say, partner?'

For what seemed like an hour, in effect little more than ten seconds, the two gunslicks held each other's gaze.

Then Mendoza smiled. He clapped his new sidekick on the shoulder.

'You are indeed welcome to join the Red River crew, Banner my friend,' he enthused with vigour. 'And I am sure that now you are the *amigo* of Juan Castillo de Mendoza, thee boys also weel give you a warm welcome.'

Largo sighed with relief, letting his breath out silently. He had succeeded in convincing Mendoza that he was genuine. The others would surely be a pushover.

With a whoop of delight, Mendoza set his sombrero straight and spurred down the loose gradient with Largo following at a more sedate pace.

9

The Del Macho Sink

On the canyon floor it was hot enough to melt the eyes of a prairie dog. Red dust devils twisted and frolicked like a chorus of erotic dancers. And through the whirling haze, Largo could just discern four men standing outside the cabin awaiting his arrival. The only animated figure was Mendoza, pointing and gesticulating wildly. He had galloped ahead anxious to surprise his *compadres*.

As Largo drew nearer to the small group of coldblooded outlaws, the less welcoming they appeared. In fact, they looked positively hostile, even aggressive. Mendoza hurried across ready to introduce his new associate. He was in an excited frame of mind.

At that moment, a young Indian

squaw appeared. Her languid profile was framed in the cabin door. Long black hair cascaded down her back held in place by a red bandanna. From the cut of her buckskin shift, Largo judged her to be Kiowa. And she was a stunner. Even from that distance there was no doubting her natural beauty. Through the shapeless smock he could tell she boasted a striking figure.

Mendoza instantly picked up on his partner's fascination.

'You best not have any ideas where Conchita is concerned, *amigo*,' he warned. 'She ees Cantrell's *muchacha*. Bought and paid for. Others have sought to take her from him. They are no more.' He made an obvious chopping gesture across his throat. 'You understand?'

Largo remained silent, his craggy features impenetrable.

A slave girl!

He had heard about Indian squaws being captured by other tribes and then sold into bondage to the highest bidder.

But this was the first time he had encountered the practice. It brought a lump to his throat. To treat other human beings as simple chattels had always been anathema to him. A barbaric practice that needed stamping out. That was one reason why he had forsaken his own state's sympathies to join forces with the North in the fight against just such injustice.

But this was no time to voice his disquiet.

'What do we know about this jasper?' barked a burly six footer. Largo recognized him as Rufe Claybourne. A more hot-headed bruiser was difficult to imagine. The guy was far more brutish in the flesh than his wanted dodger suggested.

'Yeh!' agreed a little weasel. Mangas Pete was picking his dirty fingernails with a huge ten-inch bowie knife. In his hands it looked like a cavalry sabre. 'We don't need no extra guns. It only cuts down the *dinero* for the rest of us.'

'But he is a good fellow, *amigos*,'

pressed Mendoza, gesturing for his new *compañero* to join them. 'And any man who rescues Juan de Mendoza from thee gallows, then shoots hees captor, ees a hero in my eyes.' The Mexican drew himself up challenging the others, grimacing fiercely at each in turn. 'What you say, Cherokee?'

The statuesque Indian merely grunted. His angular face, brittle and stoically impassive, stared coldly at the newcomer.

'George always go with the boss.' The deep crusty tone was brief and to the point.

The gang members turned as one to their leader for his decision.

Texas Jack had been studying the newcomer closely. Leaning against the door post, thumbs hooked into twin gun belts, his lips parted in a hollow grin. Slowly he walked over to Largo and stood facing him.

Quick as a flash, his hand rose and slapped the bounty-hunter across the face. Even before the echo of the harsh crack had died, the barrel of a cocked

Frontier was jabbing at his throat. Largo fastened a stiff eye onto the gang boss. Cantrell's own hard look was unflinching.

There was a sharp intake of breath from the assembled outlaws. They waited, tense and overawed by this sudden shift in fortunes. All it needed was a slight twitch of a trigger finger and their boss would be blasted to hell.

Then a harsh chortle issued from Cantrell's pursed lips. He stepped back away from the threatening pistol, took out a cigar and handed it to Largo. The bounty-hunter slowly holstered his piece and accepted the offering and the lighted match.

'This guy's OK. He's got guts,' said the man in black, puffing on his own smoke. 'Any feller who'd take a slap like that ain't worth a wooden dime to me. And the man who rescues Dogface and guns down a sheriff in the process has to be taken seriously.'

Mendoza stiffened, flinching momentarily. Only Jack Cantrell could call the

Mexican by his reviled nickname to his face and escape unscathed.

'What did I say, Banner, my good friend,' he enthused flinging an arm round Largo's shoulder. 'The boys, they welcome you with open arms.' He then led the way back to the cabin. 'Let us celebrate with a drink or two, or maybe even three.' Mendoza laughed, raising a bottle in salute. 'To my rescue and my new *compadre*.'

Rufe Claybourne held back, nudging Cantrell aside.

'I don't trust this jigger, boss,' he hissed. 'Too danged convenient, him just happenin' on that sheriff by accident.'

Cantrell's eyes narrowed, a dark cast shadowing his face. His next words were low and menacing. 'Then keep yer peepers on him. Watch his every move. And if'n he puts one foot outa line, you got my permission to skin him alive. But until then, he's one of us. Savvy?'

'Sure thing, boss.'

Over the next few days, Largo — now known as Banner — settled into the easy-going routine of the camp. He knew that Cantrell was planning another big job. The gang boss had hinted as much. But so far he had kept the gist of the caper to himself. Even Mendoza, who had resumed his position as second-in-command, was not privy to the details.

Texas Jack was always like this before a job, the Mexican had informed Largo when he had casually mentioned the notion. Works things out in his head to begin with and only divulges the details to the gang just before they light out. That way there was no chance of anyone letting anything slip if they visit a town.

The nearest settlement that Cantrell allowed his men to visit, Largo discovered, was two days' ride to the northeast. Fort Sumner was closer, but out of bounds for obvious reasons. Clambake was little more than a few shacks surrounding a trading post. Sometimes, a couple of the boys would ride over there for some action if their peckers became a little itchy. Mendoza uttered a dirty laugh. Not for him the soiled doves of some hick frontier burg. He would wait until he could buy himself some classy dame in Santa Fe.

'We do thees thing together, eh Banner?' he gushed, one night, after sinking almost a full bottle of best Scotch whisky. His voice was becoming slurred. 'You my good *amigo*. I share everytheenk with my friend. Even my women.' That notion propelled him into unrestrained laughter.

'What's wrong with Clambake then?' asked Largo, 'I could fancy visitin' a town if Cantrell is gonna keep us here much longer.' Trying to maintain a blasé nuance in his voice, he enquired, 'Do they have a telegraph office there?'

'Too small for that,' replied Mendoza shaking his head. 'Why you ask?'

'No reason. Just wonderin' is all.' Largo disguised the slight catch in his gruff response by clearing his throat, accurately hawking the contents of his mouth into a corner spittoon.

They had been sitting on the veranda. It was evening time. The intense heat of the day had faded. Inside the cabin, Cantrell had been busy scratching notes on a pad. Any attempt to draw him into their conversation had been met by a brusque rebuttal. Mendoza had confided to his new comrade that this was always the boss's reaction when he was planning a new job.

Largo had just finished oiling and cleaning the Colt Frontier, checking the action was tight and certain when the door opened.

It was Claybourne.

'Boss wants you inside,' he said curtly, addressing them both.

When Largo didn't immediately jump to his feet, Claybourne snorted, 'That means now, mister. Not next week.'

The new man ignored the jibe. A lazy

smile creased his face as the big hardcase fumed impotently. With deliberate apathy, he reassembled the revolver then casually stood up, nonchalantly shouldering through the door to join the others.

Cantrell was seated at the table with Conchita immediately behind. Her hand rested on his shoulder. The half smile was cold, fixed and muted. A deep sadness enveloped her whole being. Large round eyes shaded a brilliant azure appeared flat and inert, devoid of life. The others appeared not to notice. Perhaps they were used to Conchita's presence. Only Largo sensed the girl's pain, her humiliation.

Cherokee George was the last to arrive. He had been on lookout perched high atop the rocky knoll overlooking the valley, something Cantrell always insisted upon, even in this supposedly secret locale.

Once the whole gang had assembled, Cantrell outlined the plan he had worked out for their next job.

'We're gonna do the biggest bank this side of the Big Muddy.' His dark eyes glittered beneath hooded brows. He looked at each of them in turn, smirking at their stunned expressions. 'And that's the First National in the town of Manassas. My information is there'll be upwards of fifty grand in the vault next week. So we gotta move fast.'

'But that ain't no swanky town, boss,' piped up Mangas Pete, expressing what the others also had in mind. 'So how come it has the biggest haul?'

Cantrell tapped his nose conspiratorially.

'Now that's where the bank officials have been real cute,' he smirked. 'They've allus proclaimed the one in Contention is their head office. Maybe it is. But the vast bulk of the *dinero* is stashed away in Manassas. It's a trick to stymie guys like us.' The gang leader gave a mirthless guffaw stabbing a thumb at his chest with evident pride. 'No sirree. Them clever greenhorns didn't figure on havin' to deal with

Texas Jack Cantrell. So that's what we're gonna hit. I'll sort out the details of what each of you has to do on the trail.'

At this he pushed back his chair and stood up, grabbed a waiting glass of tequila from the hovering Conchita, and tipped it down his throat in one. The fiery spirit brought a red flush to his gaunt face. Then, taking hold of the girl's arm, he headed for the back room that he had commandeered for his own personal use. Just one of the perks of being a gang boss, plus the night-time entertainment. The others had to make do with sharing the two bunk beds or sleeping in the adjacent barn.

Pausing in the doorway, Cantrell declared, 'You boys would be advised to get some shut-eye. We'll be headin' out at first light.'

★　★　★

Following a breakfast of tortillas and refried beans washed down with thick black coffee prepared by Conchita, the gang saddled up and pulled out. The girl had been left behind. She was standing in the doorway, just like when Largo had first arrived at the hideout. But without a horse, there was no chance of her escaping the clutches of her master.

She had tried it once before. For three days she had been hunted like a beast of the forest. The physical marks of the beating she had received from her crazed master had long since healed. But the livid scars seared onto her mind would never fade. Someday, Conchita, daughter of the great Kiowa medicine man, White Bear, would have her revenge.

Since Largo's arrival five days before, Conchita had uttered not a single word. At least not in Largo's presence. Her purpose was merely to serve and be used. And with a body as alluring as hers, it was obvious to any red-blooded male exactly what that usage would be.

As the six riders trotted away from

the cabin, Largo was the only member of the gang to look back. His eyes locked onto Conchita's haunted demeanour, silently trying to convey his empathy and support, willing her to recognize that he was different, not some mean-eyed desperado on the make. An ally amidst this nest of scavenging vipers.

Whether or not she cottoned to his fervent supplication, Largo had no way of ascertaining. The girl remained immobile, impassive, her true feelings hidden behind a blank mask. And so she remained until the cabin had disappeared from their view behind a surging butte of red sandstone known as the Quivera Steeple.

Around noon, Cantrell called a halt. Mangas Pete set to work lighting a fire and preparing a pot of coffee. The others stretched their tired and aching muscles. Six hours in the saddle is apt to tenderize the toughest posterior. Once the mugs were filled with the steaming brew, the weasel handed out freshly baked biscuits prepared by their Indian captive.

'This sure is a heap better 'n your crabby victuals, Pete,' snorted Rufe Claybourne through a mouthful of the tasty repast.

The others chortled in agreement. Even Cherokee George could see the funny side.

'Weasel-face, he truly no top cooker,' the Indian snickered laconically.

The little man took it all in good part. He was used to such joshing, and actually enjoyed the task of being camp supremo when they were on the move. He threw some crumbs to a group of soldier ants, then sat mesmerised by their antics of trying to carry off this unexpected prize.

'Yeh!' continued Claybourne pulling hard on a thin stogie. 'That gal is more'n just a roll in the hay, ain't that the goldarned truth.'

A heavy silence fell over the small gathering. Mouths ceased their chewing, eyes swivelled to Jack Cantrell. The boss leapt to his feet. A venomous look, black as coal, fastened onto the hot-head spearing him to the spot. Instantly, Claybourne knew he had gone too far. Desperately he tried to backtrack.

'Didn't mean no offence, boss,' he whined, fear clearly registering across his pinched visage. 'It just slipped out.'

With no hesitation, Cantrell struck the cringing bruiser a stiff backhander across the mouth. Blood seeped from the edges of the cut lip dribbling down into the unkempt beard. Claybourne fell to the ground, his hand automatically reaching for the pistol on his hip.

But Cantrell's was already aimed at his head.

'Keep yer goddamned slimy comments to yerself, mister,' he growled, standing over the big man, every syllable discharging dire retribution should the advice not be heeded. 'You got that?'

'S-sure thing, boss,' stammered Claybourne, looking away to hide his humiliation.

Cantrell was well aware that he needed all his men on this raid. So he hurried on to avoid any resentment festering in Claybourne's warped mind.

'Now listen up, boys,' he announced, quickly, changing tack, his voice laced with keen anticipation. 'This is how the Red River Gang make the biggest haul so far in its brief but profitable history.' The others gathered round expectantly, their eyes glittering with avarice. Even Rufe Claybourne perked up, putting the acquisition of ready cash ahead of any personal resentment. 'And after this one, we'll split up and go our separate ways.'

'You mean thees will be our last job?' asked a stunned Mendoza.

'Until I think it wise to start up again.'

'And when might that be?' butted in the new man. Largo knew now that this would be his and Kyte's only chance to nail the gang. He would have to get word to the older man. And soon.

'Six months, a year,' responded

Cantrell, shrugging. He stroked his thick sweeping moustache thoughtfully before adding, 'Depends on when the dough runs out.'

He then went on to explain the plan he had worked out. It basically followed the same format as previously. Largo would take the place of the deceased Slim Brewster, with the recently freed Dogface Mendoza once again assuming his rightful place alongside the boss.

*   *   *

By late afternoon, the group of dust-shrouded riders were nearing the town of Buckeye. It was an old Indian pueblo at the foot of the escarpment that fronted the soaring Conejos Mesa. Although sheltered from the merciless onslaught of the incessant heat and occupying a fertile valley, it lacked that most basic of requirements — natural defence from other warring tribes. Unable to contain the increasingly frequent and successful raids on their homes, the Indians had been forced to abandon Conejos and move away.

The recent discovery of copper in the vicinity had led to the town's resurrection. It had emerged from obscurity becoming a thriving settlement. There was even rumour of a branch line from the Southern Pacific being directed here in the not too distant future.

Renamed Buckeye on account of the rampant proliferation of rabbit colonies amidst the crumbling dwellings, the town was approximately halfway *en route* to the gang's destination; an ideal resting point before the final push across the dry wasteland known as the Devil's Playground. And it was well named. Not a drop of water for thirty miles, nor even a blade of grass. Here was a desert where even the ubiquitous buzzard hesitated before making its presence felt.

Cantrell cast a thoughtful eye towards the sandy wilderness that stretched to the distant horizon on the far side of the town. It was now Friday. And the gang boss knew that the bank at Manassas would be chock-full of cash by the middle of the following week. That should give them ample time to make their preparations ready for an early start the following day.

That desert was gonna take some crossing.

10

Buckeye

Nudging their horses down the main street of Buckeye, Cantrell cast a jaundiced eye over the settlement. It was no boom town on a par with the gold and silver mining camps where prospectors flooded in *en masse* to stake their claims, not to mention the blood-sucking leeches who preyed on their good fortune. Copper did not have that allure. Only large conglomerates operated in such places. And the excavated ore was quickly freighted out in long ox-drawn wagon trains.

Interspersed with an array of grubby tents, wooden false-fronted buildings had taken root lining both sides of the wide street. As yet there were no solid brick-built structures to lend an air of permanence to the town. It was as if the place was awaiting something concrete to ensure its claim to stability. After all, if the copper ceased to be economically viable, Buckeye would go the way of a thousand other boom and bust settlements that littered the West.

Largo avidly studied the layout of the town, his anxious gaze probing the various establishments as the gang casually sauntered along the main street. Then he saw it. A tiny shack with no signboard announcing its purpose, but the adjacent pole with connecting wires said it all.

The telegraph office!

Largo's eyes lit up. His granite features, however, remained taciturn, devoid of expression as he continued staring straight ahead.

The six riders attracted little curiosity. Only a flea-bitten mutt idly pursuing a clump of tumbleweed ceased its play to glower at the newcomers. After all, there was no money stashed here worth the robbing. It all ended up in the bank at

Contention. Or so the local populace assumed.

Hauling rein in front of a saloon boasting the inviting appellation of Diamond Lil's Stocking Top, they tied off their mounts to the hitching rail and elbowed the batwings aside. All of them were grateful for the coolness of the interior and anxious to wash the trail dust from dried-up throats. Largo was no exception.

The place was crowded. Others clearly had the same notion. A raucous hubbub assailed the senses. Dirty straw to soak up spilled ale covered the floor. Smoky and reeking of stale beer and unwashed bodies, the place bore little relation to an alluring boudoir suggestive of the name stamped on the outside.

Mendoza was first through the door. Almost foaming at the mouth, his gaze searched greedily for the lady in question, not to mention the enticing portions of her anatomy on public display. His fervid gaze cut through the thick atmosphere, searching. But all he could discern were the usual frowsty saloon gals trying to catch his eye.

Then he saw her. Immediately in front. Splayed out in all her glory and dressed to kill: the enigmatic Diamond Lil. Except it wasn't the lady herself in the flesh, but merely a large painted cut-out nailed to the wall. Mendoza felt he had been cheated. His swarthy complexion took on a purple hue. His hand dropped to the revolver on his hip. The release of angry frustration was to riddle this odious caricature with a hail of bullets.

Judging by the number of holes already in the colourful effigy, he was not the first client to feel duped. The saloon's erotically tempting name was there purely to draw the punters inside. Quick to note his sidekick's threatening response to the slight, Cantrell laid a cautionary hand on his arm.

'Cool it, Dogface,' he hissed out the side of his mouth. 'The last thing we want now is to draw attention to our-selves.'

The Mexican emitted a petulant growl of hurt pride. This was a question of *machismo*. He strained to haul out his piece, but Cantrell maintained a tight grip.

'I said simmer down,' he rasped acidly.

The moment for blind retaliation had passed. Mendoza's face lost its brassy edge. He muttered some choice epithets incoherently in his own tongue, then shrugged off the restraining hand and stalked over to the bar.

It was some ten minutes later that Largo felt a tug on the sleeve of his shirt.

'Remember me then, mister?' chirped a shortish dude of rotund appearance clutching a glass of beer.

Largo stiffened, but ignored the newcomer. He took another sip of his beer casually flicking a wary eye over the hovering porker.

'Carlsbad Junction,' continued the man unabashed. 'Did you manage to catch up with that bad ass at Alamagordo?' Henry Tasker scratched his balding pate. 'What was his name ... ? Hambone Walker, that was it.'

Setting his pot down, Largo had no choice but to address this unwelcome intruder.

'You must be mistaken, feller,' he drawled, trying to sound casual and unhurried. 'Never been to Carlsbad. And who might Hambone Walker be?'

'An outlaw you was trailin' after,' insisted Tasker, settling his round beady gaze on the big man. 'Eight hundred bucks reward if I recall right.'

By now, the other members of the gang were all ears, their drinks forgotten.

Largo had to take the initiative else this interfering bastard was gonna blow his cover sky high. Without any further preamble, he swung round and grabbed the little guy, hoisting him off his feet.

'Now listen up good, fat boy,' he snarled, shaking the guy as if he was churning butter, 'I don't know you. Ain't never seen yuh afore. So leave me alone. Got that?'

'S-sorry, m-mister,' stammered the frightened depot clerk from between rattling teeth. 'Anybody c-can make a m-mistake.'

Skewering the quaking intruder with the evil eye, Largo released him and turned back to the bar desperately attempting to salvage his newly acquired status as a hardened desperado.

'What was all that about?' asked Cantrell, suspicion writ deeply into his ribbed features. 'Some'n about a reward fer takin' out Hambone Walker.'

'Ignore the guy, Jack. Too much booze. He's seein' things what ain't there.'

'Sounds perty damn shifty to me,' railed Mangas Pete, stroking the bone handle of his sheathed bowie.

'I tell yuh the guy's mistaken,' stressed Largo vehemently. 'It's happened before. There must be some rannie out there what's my double. If I ever find the critter, I'll string him up myself.'

Such was the new boy's insistence

that he was the victim of mistaken identity, that Cantrell gave him the benefit of the doubt.

Mendoza likewise was more than willing to lend support to his new *compadre*. 'I too haf been meestaken for someone else,' he averred. 'Banner ees good *hombre*. Anybody who keels thee sheriff and rescues me ees welcome in thee Red River Gang as far as Juan Castillo de Mendoza is concerned.'

Following that endorsement, the tension eased palpably. Largo slowly relaxed. A thin trickle of cold sweat traced a path down his spine reminding him that life as a bounty-hunter was never cut and dried. That was close, he mused. Real close.

But there was one guy who was not convinced of Largo's veracity. Rufe Claybourne's icy glower threatened dire consequences should his suspicions be proved correct.

Huddling over his drink, Largo knew that he had to get a message to

Sebastian Kyte in Fort Sumner telling him of the imminent raid on the bank at Manassas. And that telegraph office was the key. He gave it another fifteen minutes when the drinks were flowing. Mangas Pete and Cherokee George had gone off to shoot some craps. Mendoza had recovered his macho image by chatting up one of the less slatternly girls on offer. Only Cantrell and Rufe Claybourne were still at the bar.

'That cayuse of mine was strugglin' a mite on that last down grade,' announced Largo to the gang boss. 'Figure I'll look me out a livery man to check her out.'

'Want some company,' offered Cantrell easily, the previous incident apparently forgotten.

'No need,' replied Largo rather too quickly.

'Suit yerself.'

Shrugging away from the bar, Largo set his hat and headed for the door. Once outside he hurried away in the direction of the telegraph office. Covertly, he cast a wary eye behind him to ensure nobody was following. His destination was on the far side of the street, 100 yards to the south. Stopping short of the small shack, he cast another wary look around then stepped inside quickly. The telegraph clerk was hammering away at the morse key.

Largo selected an official form and wrote down in block capitals the short but succinct message that read: COLONEL. ACCEPTED BY COMPANY. JOB AT MANASSAS. START WEDNESDAY AM. LARGO. Reading the message back to himself, Largo gave a satisfied nod. Only Seb Kyte would know he was referring to a bank raid. To all intents and purposes the message was an innocent one concerning employment.

Who would suspect otherwise? It was now Friday. Plenty of time for the older man to reach Manassas and contact the local tin star to arrange an ambush.

Finally the clerk finished his current

task and turned to address the newcomer.

'What'll it be then, mister?' he said brightly.

Largo handed him the note.

'Does this go direct to Fort Sumner?' he asked.

'As direct as the lines will allow,' quipped the clerk, as he went to work. 'Great invention the telegraph,' he added, fingers buzzing with controlled expertise. 'This message will be at Fort Sumner quicker'n you was a-writin' it out.'

'That's just what I was hopin' fer,' smiled Largo. He then paid the dispatch fee and left.

Once outside in the street, Largo took hold of Dancer's lead rein and continued further down in search of a livery stable. The ruse had to be followed through.

All that the ostler found was a rather deep cut on the horse's left foreleg. He cleaned it up and applied an antiseptic salve, charging fifty cents for the service.

Wandering back up the street a half-hour later, Largo noticed Mendoza on the far side. He was pointing to a narrow gunnel running between a gunsmith's emporium and a dressmaker's. The Mexican was gesturing for Largo to follow him down. He surmised it must have something to do with preparations for the upcoming venture. Within the confines of the passage, dark shadows blocked out the lowering sun. Mendoza had disappeared. He must be round the back.

Turning the corner at the end, a heavy weight crashed into Largo's back propelling him against a water butt. Arms outstretched to break his fall, his stunned mind was given no time to recover. The ambush had taken him completely by surprise. The bushwhackers quickly followed up their attack with a flurry of well-directed punches that peppered his exposed face and body.

Largo was barely able to defend himself. The jabber of agonizing blows seemed endless, each selected to deliver maximum damage and pain. All he could do was try to fend off those aiming for his more vital areas. Sharp grunts accompanied the incessant welter of blows as boots and tightly clenched fists all did their job with ruthless efficiency. These bastards were no amateurs. There was no time even to cry out, to protest his innocence. A red mist of agony flooded his brain. Consciousness was fast slipping away.

All of a sudden, the rain of savage punches ceased. Forcing open a rapidly swelling eye, all he could see was the glowering face of Rufe Claybourne. Through the opaque haziness, Largo knew that his cover had been blown. There was no point in denying it.

But how? Then he remembered: the unfortunate meeting with Henry Tasker, the railway depot clerk. That had to be it. He was given no time to ponder on the dilemma. Mangas dragged him upright. But not for long.

His head was plunged into the water

butt. The dousing momentarily cleared his frazzled brain, but only to realize the true enormity of his situation. Were they going to drown him? His lungs felt like they were about to burst. In such circumstances, the instinct for survival takes control, a frantic desperation to thwart the inexorable onset of death. But Largo's mind was beginning to fade, the strength quickly ebbing from weary muscles.

Just when it appeared that the grim reaper was calling his name, his head was pulled clear. Water poured from his open mouth as he desperately gulped in fresh air. From faraway an abrasive voice grated on his wilting sensibility, a razor-sharp knife pricking the exposed skin of his neck. It was the acute pain that brought him lumbering back to the grim reality of his situation.

With infinite slowness his gritty red-rimmed eyes flickered open. Racked by a thousand agonizing jolts, all he wanted was the blessed relief of darkness to enfold his tormented limbs.

But it was not to be.

He was securely pinioned by three of the Red River boys. Like a manic gnome, Mangas Pete pranced around jabbing at him with the knife. Immediately in front stood Jack Cantrell, an ugly smile pasted across the seamed visage. Idly, almost lovingly, he caressed one of his hoglegs, Largo's blood dripping from the barrel.

The bounty-hunter's aching head lolled on slumped shoulders. He hadn't even the strength to raise up and meet the unflinching stare of his tormentor. It was Rufe Claybourne who made the next move, grabbing his long hair and yanking back, almost tearing his head from his body. Largo winced but still managed to hold the gang leader's gaze.

'So, Mr Banner,' smirked Cantrell, 'or should I call you Largo?'

The bruised captive stiffened. So they knew his real name.

'Was it Tasker?'

'Tasker?' queried Cantrell.

'The dude in the saloon.' Largo's

words were slurred, broken, just like the mashed lips that were beginning to swell and discolour. 'Him what recognized me.'

Cantrell shook his head. 'Rufe here didn't trust you from the very start.'

'Neither did I,' piped up Mangas.

Cantrell's next comment, snappy and with a barbed edge, was aimed at Dogface Mendoza. 'Unlike this greaseball who was taken in like a hooked trout.'

'What would you do eef some *hombre* saved you from thee hangman's noose?' retorted the Mexican in a lilting whine. 'Ask for hees credentials?'

Cantrell ignored the interruption.

'And I don't accept nobody's word until they prove themselves. This bank job in Manassas was your chance to do just that. You blew it, mister.' A back-handed crack to the jaw rattled Largo's teeth. Cantrell's thin lips drew back in an evil grin as he lit up a cheroot. 'I had Rufe here follow you down to the telegraph office.' A tight smile cracked the icy demeanour. 'The guy has a way of persuading folks to part with information. Ain't that the case, Rufe?'

'Sure is, boss.'

'So now we know the truth of the matter. At this very moment, your partner will be headin' for Manassas to organize a reception party to meet us outside the bank.'

The gang boss smiled again as he paused for effect. He didn't seem bothered. Drawing hard on the cigar, he funnelled a tube of blue smoke at Largo's damaged face. The puzzled reaction brought on a savage laugh. A maniacal howl that was fiercesome in its ardour.

Quickly regaining control, Cantrell continued, 'Your partner is gonna be mightily disappointed.'

'Why's that?' queried Largo.

''Cos it's the bank in Contention we're actually gonna hit.' The others joined in with another bout of rabid guffawing. 'All them there lawdogs hightailin' it over to Manassas allowin' us to just ride in to Contention and clear up. What d'yuh say to that then, *Mister* Largo?'

The bounty-hunter was dumbfounded, lost for words. He had been outfoxed by a bunch of dumb-ass owlhooters. Not so stupid after all. And for his patronizing arrogance, he would doubtless pay the ultimate price.

'What we gonna do with this piece of dog shit then, boss?' asked Mangas Pete waving the large bowie under Largo's nose. 'Should I slit his gizzard here and now?'

Cantrell's thick brows creased in thought.

'Not yet awhile,' he proposed, 'Cherokee George can take him back to the hideout and lock him up in the dugout until we get back from this caper. That'll give the varmint plenty of time to figure out how we're gonna finish him off. Make you sweat a little, Mr Largo. 'Sides, we don't wanna leave no dead bodies lyin' around here.

Might cause awkward questions.'

While the Indian was securely tethering Largo to his horse, Cantrell gave him his final instructions.

'Take the old Mescalero trail through the mountains. That way you won't bump into anybody. Meet us at Spider Rock soon as you can, then we'll head fer the river crossing at Bittersweet.' As a postscript he added, 'And bring the girl. No point givin' her ideas where this rannie's concerned.'

George gave a curt nod then spurred off, trailing Largo and Dancer behind. Circling the chaotic huddle of back lots, they were soon lost to view.

11

Kiowa Medicine

Cherokee George knew every trail that criss-crossed the complexity of broken canyons that made up the Del Macho Sink. It was an intimacy gained through hard and often painful experience. As a youngster barely above the age of puberty, he had survived the harsh rigors of tribal apprenticeship thereby earning the right to bear arms as a fully fledged Cherokee brave. That was the proudest moment of his life.

In the early years, life for a young Cherokee was both rewarding and exciting. And so it would have continued but for the constant incursions into their tribal lands by the hated white eyes. Like a cancerous growth, the invaders had gnawed away at the landscape taking more and more of the land for their own purposes, invariably associated with the yellow metal they so desperately coveted.

The final insult came when a drunken settler raped his mother. Eagle Swoops Low, as he was then called, had little faith that the white-man's justice would prevail. And so it had proved. The culprit was released to continue his vile attacks. Always prone to impetuous and often reckless action, he scorned the calming influence of the tribal elders branding them weak-willed old women. The only possible course of action was to hunt the man down and render his own form of justice.

Once caught, it had taken the man three days before he finally sank into blessed oblivion. And from that day onwards, Eagle Swoops Low was a marked man.

He teamed up with Texas Jack Cantrell by accident after another hardcase known as Two Bits Rankin had stolen the gang leader's woman. That was before he bought Conchita.

When Two Bits started baiting the Cherokee in a Las Cruces saloon, Cantrell saw an excuse to take revenge.

His Colt .45 did the talking.

Eagle Swoops Low was taken on by Cantrell as a sort of mascot, a lucky totem. From that day forward he was referred to as Cherokee George, his tribal name being too much of a mouthful for the simple fools who inhabited the white-man's world. George accepted the situation and became an indispensable member of the Red River Gang.

The trek back into the labyrinthine badlands that comprised the Del Macho Sink was a nightmarish daze for Largo. Each jog of his horse sent barbs of agony through his tormented frame. Even had his battered wits remained acute, Largo could never have memorized the course of the trail that Cherokee George was following. Like all Indians who considered themselves at one with nature, George had an innate sense of direction, a natural affinity for the land handed down through generations of tribal inheritance.

Eventually the cabin hove into view.

Conchita came out onto the veranda. She could not fail to notice the beating to which Largo had been subjected. Their eyes met. The girl remained impassive, untouched by the hideous sight of a fellow human being in obvious torment. Maybe that was the Indian way, pain and suffering an endemic fact of life.

George dragged the pinioned captive from his mount and hustled him over to the far side of the cabin. Pulling on a rope, he opened a trapdoor that revealed a hollowed out chamber in the ground some ten feet square and of similar depth. A ladder led down into the gloomy entrails. This was the dugout mentioned by Cantrell. Intended as a cooling larder to keep fresh meat and other perishables from rotting in the hot climate, it also doubled up as a first rate dungeon.

'You go down,' boomed George in a clipped accent, emphasizing the order with his rifle.

'What about these?' Largo raised his bound hands. 'I can't climb down there like this.'

'Go!'

Cherokee George's verbal output was nothing if not concise. His rifle jabbing into Largo's stomach was much more persuasive.

The prisoner gagged, stumbling against the upright trap. Already severely weakened and lacking balance, his boot slid over the edge of the hole. With hands tied and no means of support, he tumbled headlong down into the black pit. A heavy thud was followed by an agonized groan.

A throaty gurgle meant as a laugh followed him as the Cherokee hauled up the ladder and slammed the trap down, securing it with a bolt.

It was Largo's good fortune that the dirt floor was filled with sacks of dried pinto beans to cushion his fall. Without them, he could have easily broken a leg, or worse — if things could get any worse, that is. At that precise moment, he very much doubted it. Then again, he hadn't suffered any permanent injury. A nasty beating to be sure, but thankfully sustaining only superficial cuts and bruises.

The only light in the subterranean prison lanced down through a crack in the trapdoor. As the hours slowly passed, the thin beam arced across the dirt walls. Eventually, through sheer exhaustion, the prisoner fell asleep.

Almost immediately a scraping above jerked him awake. The trapdoor swung open. Purple and pink striations daubed across the overhead canopy informed him that it was early evening. He must have been asleep over five hours. The enforced rest had done him good. Still exceedingly stiff and with aching muscles that jarred at the slightest movement, at least his mind was alert.

A figure was silhouetted against the vivid backdrop. It was the Indian girl.

She was lowering a basket down on a rope.

'Food,' she said in a surprisingly soft voice. 'You eat now. There is knife in basket.' Furtively she cast a nervous glance back towards the cabin. Then, in a halting whisper added, 'Later, I come for you.'

Largo's heart jumped. So Conchita was going to help him. Had even provided a blade to cut himself free. He could only pray that she would somehow manage to disable the 'breed and put him out of action.

But how?

'What yuh gonna do?'

'No tell now. George get suspicious.'

'You be careful now.' There was concern in Largo's edgy tone, and not just for himself. 'That 'breed is one savage critter.'

His mind chilled with dread on recalling Cherokee George's lurid details of the slow and agonizing death he was going to suffer when the gang returned from having completed the Contention robbery. An involuntarily spine-tingling shudder racked his tormented body at the memory.

The hint of a smile broke across the Kiowa squaw's oval face. It was the first time Largo had witnessed such a show of emotion. The transformation was a breath of fresh air, her whole demeanour shone like a beacon of light. Then the trapdoor banged shut and she was gone.

Quickly he took hold of the knife with both hands and sawed at the thick bonds. The razor-edged blade sliced through the hemp in no time. Hot chilli beans and corn bread infused a new strength into his aching limbs.

When the girl returned, he would be ready.

★   ★   ★

'Where you been?' demanded the 'breed when Conchita returned to the cabin. He was sat at the table wolfing down his own food noisily.

184

'Feeding prisoner,' she responded curtly.

George grunted, wiping the rich gravy from his grease-smeared mouth.

'Why you waste good food on him?' Dark eyes crinkled in an ugly leer. 'He soon be feeding ants.'

'You drink,' said Conchita, ignoring the question and pouring a generous measure of whiskey into a tin mug. She stood watching him. There was a restless air about her posture, a tenseness she felt certain he would notice. But Cherokee George had eyes only for the amber liquid.

George accepted the mug, slurping greedily. The whiteman's fire water was far better than anything his own tribe had ever brewed. He coughed as the harsh spirit grabbed at his throat.

'Taste strange,' he queried, arrowing a suspicious frown at the girl. 'Not usual drink.'

'This best stuff from Texas Jack's private stock.' The hoarse rasp was the product of nervous anxiety. 'It called

Scotch from over the big water far away.'

'Boss not like me taking his fire water,' wavered George hesitantly.

'Only one bottle,' pressed Conchita topping up the mug. Her piercing gaze willed him to drink. 'He not know. I not tell.'

The Indian considered pensively. Best Scotch; just one bottle — why not?

George tipped the rest of the mug down his throat. It really was good stuff.

Had he given the situation more thought, he might have wondered why Conchita was hovering at his elbow ever ready to top up his mug with the potent brew. But his mind was wandering, the whiskey addling his brain.

And much more besides.

The end came suddenly. One second, he was burbling on, extolling the virtues of Jack Cantrell and how the gang leader had stood up for him, the next he was crying out in agony and clutching at his stomach. An anguished howl rent the air as George tumbled off the chair rolling about on the floor. His swarthy face had turned a violent red, eyes bulging in panic. Blood seeped from between clenched teeth.

'Help me!' he pleaded, reaching out to the girl.

Conchita's reaction was a harsh peal of laughter. Savagely, she kicked him in the ribs.

'I help you into grave,' she railed, uttering a wolfish snarl as another brutal kick drove into the half-breed's quivering torso. 'You traitor. Insult all Indians.'

There was a puzzled look of bewilderment on the Cherokee's twisted visage.

The girl stood over him, hands on hips, hovering like a predatory eagle.

'That brew is special all right.' She nodded vigorously, then spat out, 'Special *poison* brew!'

George gagged as the fatal potion squeezed his innards. He began to shake violently like a dancing puppet. Suddenly, his whole body stiffened, the muscles locked tight, a final choking gasp and he left to join his ancestors. For a full minute, Conchita stared at the still corpse. Her heart beat out a pounding tattoo, bloodshot eyes dilating as the tension eased. After all these months, she was at last free of the hated bondage.

Even from the confines of his prison, Largo could clearly discern the Indian girl's frenzied shrieking. He could only pray and trust that Cherokee George was on the receiving end of her wrath and not the other way round. All he could do was wait.

Darkness had claimed the land by the time Conchita raised the trapdoor and dropped the wooden ladder for him to climb out.

His stiff muscles protested vehemently at the sudden movement. Slowly he mounted the ladder. Wobbly legs initially threatened to give way, forcing him to cling onto Conchita for support. The girl was no weakling and held him firmly.

Her closeness, the warmth of her breathing on his stubbly cheek, even the musky aroma, transformed this Indian saviour into a highly desirable woman. He clung onto her, enjoying the proximity, the intimacy of the contact. It was a sensation alien to his nature. A hard-nosed bounty-hunter took his pleasures where he found them, satisfying his innermost needs then moving on.

This girl was different. The notion that he might have feelings for her caused him to pull away. It was an unnerving sentiment that he found hard to comprehend.

Gruffly, to hide his discomfiture, the big man mumbled, 'Yuh took care of George then?'

She nodded. 'My father, he famous Kiowa medicine man, White Bear. Taught me many things. Potions to save life; others that end it.'

Largo didn't need to ask which type the Cherokee had imbibed. An owl hooted in the distance, a sad mournful cry. Perhaps it had encountered the spirit of the dead tracker on his final journey.

Stamping around the clearing helped to stimulate the blood in Largo's veins. It also disguised the conflicting thoughts that were swimming around in his head. Conchita was experiencing a similar array of strange feelings towards this rugged stranger who had been thrust into her life.

Being a down-to-earth person, she pushed such thoughts to the back of her mind. There were other more vital concerns to be addressed. They could not stay here now. Cantrell and the rest of the gang would be back as soon as they had robbed the bank.

But first, the stranger needed her ministrations.

Taking hold of his arm she led him to the cabin, sitting him down at the table. Cherokee George stared up at him, the eyes milky and sightless in death. Conchita ignored the gruesome cadaver. Extracting a bottle from a cupboard, she poured a small measure into a glass.

'Drink!'

Largo cast a wary eye at the thick brown liquid.

'One potion for him,' — Conchita nodded to the corpse — 'another for you. Now drink!' Her tone was sympathetic but firm. At the same time she began applying a cooling ointment to the numerous cuts and abrasions that covered Largo's body.

After helping him on with his shirt, Conchita set about gathering supplies for the journey.

'We must leave soon,' she announced, whilst packing a saddle-bag. 'Rest here for one cigar smoke. Then see to horses. You do?'

Largo nodded.

Within a half-hour, they were heading back along the trail. Already, Largo could feel the aches and pains dissolving. He felt stronger, more like his old self.

'I have to reach Fort Sumner and send word to my partner,' stressed

Largo, as they passed the towering pinnacle of Quivera Steeple, now black against the fiery backdrop of impending night. 'I've sent him on a wild-goose chase over to Manassas.'

The girl drew to a halt, her hawkish gaze probing the rapidly dimming landscape.

'We ride all through night,' she said, leaving the Buckeye trail to head north along a deer run. 'Should reach fort by noon tomorrow.'

Largo could only follow in her wake. He was now totally dependent on this Kiowa squaw. It was a strange, rather confusing experience to be forced to rely on anyone else — especially such a beautiful guide as Conchita.

They settled down for the hard grind, pursuing a tortuous trail over the intervening range of low bluffs that comprised the Eastern Cibolas. Largo could only marvel at the confident manner in which the girl followed what to his untrained eye was an invisible trail. The animal run had long since faded into the broken landscape. And night was fast claiming its rightful place.

Throughout the long hours of darkness, Conchita maintained the gruelling pace, pausing only to hand out corn bread and apples. By dawn they had crossed the divide and were descending a series of meandering ledges that cut into the fractured rift of the sandstone terrain.

Sun-up revealed the starkly austere nature of the bleak wilderness that surrounded them on every side. It was a vast interconnecting network of ravines and gorges baked hard and devoid of vegetation apart from the ubiquitous prickly pear and sage brush that somehow managed to thrive in the arid terrain.

As the gradient eased, a wide valley opened up ahead, at the far end of which stood the strategically placed army settlement of Fort Sumner.

Conchita had been true to her word.

12

Fort Sumner

Largo's keen ear could just discern the steady tolling of a church bell as they entered the outer limits of the camp. It stopped after the twelfth ring. He smiled at the girl who revealed an even set of pure white teeth in return.

'You trust in Conchita, Mr Banner.' Her laugh was infectious, exhilarating. 'She never lead you astray.'

'I never doubted if for one minute,' he said, before correcting her misinformation. 'And the name is Largo. I changed it to avoid being recognized. Cantrell and his boys didn't know me personally, only by reputation as a bounty-hunter.'

Fort Sumner was one of the few crossing points along the elongated stretch of the Pecos River, and one of the main reasons for the army erecting a permanent camp there. Its strategic importance to the army in the heartland of hostile Indian country had attracted all manner of business interests and brought prosperity to this middle sector of the territory. Once merely an isolated military outpost, the fort was now a bustling town in its own right.

They were soon past the newly built stone fortifications and jogging down the main drag into the town itself.

Largo's nerves were on edge. He was desperately hoping to be in time to prevent his partner from leaving on a futile trip to Manassas. His steely gaze, narrowed and fully alert even after the punishing trek through the Del Macho, searched the busy street.

Nothing.

But Largo knew that a man of Sebastian Kyte's breeding would only stay in the best accommodation. No bug-ridden drovers' flop house for him. And there it was. Right in the centre of town, the Great Northern Hotel.

Even sporting a battered face that looked as if it had been hit by a charging bull, Largo might just have been able to escape any undue attention, but with a Kiowa squaw in tow, that was a forlorn expectation. Curiosity rather than outright antagonism had drawn a crowd of onlookers as the two riders tied their horses to the hitching rail.

Largo would have liked the girl to accompany him into the hotel in his search for Kyte but knew that any such undertaking was fraught with danger. Even in these more enlightened times following the Civil War, the Indian was still regarded as a second-class citizen in many quarters. Things were changing. But here on the western frontier, progress in that direction was slower than a desert tortoise.

'Stay close to the mounts,' he murmured, casting a wary peeper at the ogling faces. 'Any trouble, holler up loud and clear and I'll come a-runnin'.'

'Conchita no afraid. Can look after self.' The biting retort was matched by the resolute glint in her flashing eyes.

In a military settlement like Fort Sumner where animosity towards the red man was likely to be most acute, he felt decidedly ill at ease. Shrugging off the apprehensive disquiet, he strode purposefully into the hotel lobby. Numerous guests sat around reading newspapers and drinking coffee. Largo's colourful visage elicited more than a few raised eyebrows from the affluent clientele, but the visible presence of a gleaming Winchester rifle and side arm stifled any adverse comments.

On questioning the reception clerk, he was relieved to learn that Colonel Kyte had vacated his room but had not as yet checked out his baggage. He had gone to collect his horse from the livery stable but should be back soon.

Largo was about to order some much needed refreshment for himself and Conchita when a commotion outside in the street interrupted his conflab.

Recognizing the stilted tones of the Kiowa girl, he could only assume that some critter was making trouble for her. Throaty chuckles followed by aggrieved shrieks from Conchita confirmed his fears.

Silver spurs jingled loudly as he hurried outside.

Four down-at-heel range bums had surrounded the girl and were jabbing at her with their gun barrels. One grabbed her waist-length black plait and tugged viciously. A pained howl was dragged up from the girl's panic-stricken throat. She might have considered herself a tough cookie, but frontier towns were no place for a lone Indian girl, especially one as alluring as Conchita.

Largo cursed himself for leaving her to the dubious mercy of the crowd. He ought to have known better.

'Let's be havin' a taste of some Indian pussy then,' leered one of the toughs, pawing at the girl's full breasts. 'What d'yuh say, Stringbean?'

The lean jigger referred to as

Stringbean made an obscene gesture then pulled her towards a narrow alley that ran down the side of the hotel. Struggling and crying out in her own tongue, Conchita's supplications fell on deaf ears. Nobody in the crowd moved to give any assistance.

Largo snorted in disgust.

Shouldering aside the morbid voyeurs, he laid into the nearest hardcase with the butt of the Winchester. Poleaxed, the varmint slumped to the ground. The other three forgot their prize, turning to face her knight errant.

'So!' snarled an ugly jasper with jaundiced skin drawn tight across a cadaverous skull. 'We got us an Indian lover.'

'The fun's over, boys.' Largo's words were spoken quietly but with infinite menace. 'If'n y'all just leather them irons and walk away, I'll say no more about this unfortunate incident.'

'And if'n we don't?' This from a heavily built jasper sporting a black beard.

'Then you'll be chewing on a lead sandwich.'

The retort came from behind the three hard-nosed rannies. Their faces dropped. It was one thing facing down a single opponent, but not two. And with the second guy to their rear, now that was a different proposition entirely. Their blustering antagonism fragmented like the desert wind. Fear replaced the swaggering bravado.

'Now drop them hoglegs and split the breeze.' The blunt command had a militaristic intonation. Spoken by someone used to being obeyed, it had the desired effect.

One by one the pistols hit the dust. All except one.

Stringbean was less than keen to relinquish his weapon, or his prize. The .41 Colt Lightning was cocked and facing Largo who was holding the Winchester across his chest. Just like Hambone Walker at Alamagordo, the scumbag was weighing up his chances.

'You got the balls then, mister?' asked

Largo evenly. His lips parted in a terse smile.

'If he don't get you,' butted in the newcomer with compelling finality, 'then I certainly will.'

That did it. The arrogant Stringbean wilted. His gun followed the others.

'You can pick them up at the sheriff's office,' Largo called, as they slunk away.

The newcomer swung to face the crowd, now silenced and apprehensive.

'Any bunch of chicken-livered skunks that would allow a young girl to be manhandled like that deserves nothing but the foulest contempt.' The man, dressed in dark blue from head to foot, hawked derisively at their feet. 'Now get out of my sight, the lot of you.' He emphasized the curt remark with a couple of shots into the dust from one of his twin Schofields.

The street outside the Great Northern was empty inside two shakes of a dog's tail.

He then turned to the quivering Indian girl.

'You all right, miss?' The concerned enquiry was heartfelt and sincere.

Conchita offered a feeble nod. 'Thank you, sir,' she gasped.

'Don't forget my good friend Mr Largo here.'

Conchita smiled at the younger man.

'We're gonna have to stop meetin' like this,' grinned Largo widely, offering his hand to Sebastian Kyte. 'Although I gotta say, it's darned good to find yuh ain't upped stakes and headed out fer Manassas.'

'You only just caught me,' replied Kyte assuming a puzzled expression. 'Another half-hour and I would have been on the trail. Something gone wrong?'

In a more serious vein, Largo said, 'We gotta make new plans.'

Kyte gave his partner a quizzical frown. Then he shepherded the two of them into the hotel.

'You can tell me all about it over dinner.' His gaze raked the other man's discoloured visage before coming to rest on the girl. 'There would appear to be a lot that needs explaining.'

Whilst partaking of a sumptuous repast in the Grand Northern's renowned steak house, Largo informed his partner somewhat sheepishly of how he had been duped by Texas Jack Cantrell. After so easily securing the Mexican's release, he had become over confident, too sure of himself. When that depot clerk from Carlsbad Junction had recognized him, he should have waited, not been so impatient.

'And this was the result.' He stabbed a finger at his rearranged features. 'If it hadn't been for Conchita, that would have been the end of me. That Cherokee renegade made it plain as the nose on your face that my dyin' would have been slow and painful. And he and them other hellions would have enjoyed every damned minute watchin' me suffer.' He took another appreciative sip of the French wine, his hand reaching out to cover that of the girl's. She responded with a warm, almost intimate smile.

'Without her help, I'd never have been given this second chance.'

A finger then strayed to the deep cut, now scabbing over, that ran from his left ear to the corner of his mouth. It would heal but leave a permanent scar. Kyte frowned at the dark grimace that had so quickly scoured the younger man's weathered contours. But he remained silent. When a man comes that close to meeting his Maker, he doesn't need questions — just the chance to square his conscience, make peace with himself.

And so it all came out, a personal eulogy castigating the rancour and bitterness of a wasted life.

At last Largo fell silent, his head drooping.

Forking a piece of prime beef, he chewed slowly and steadily, before whispering, 'Now there's dues to be paid. And paid in full.'

Sebastian Kyte could only empathize with his young partner, knowing exactly what he meant.

Much as he would have preferred to set off in pursuit of the Red River Gang straight away, Largo knew that he needed rest badly. His body had taken a hammering. Conchita had achieved miracles, better than any sawbones. But without a good night's sleep, he would not be capable of undertaking the hard ride necessary if the Red River Gang was to be thwarted.

Kyte had already taken the opportunity to book him a room at the Grand Northern. Now he headed for the lobby to arrange something for Conchita. Unheard of in Fort Sumner's brief yet turbulent history, the announcement that he wanted a room for his Kiowa guest was met with stunned amazement by the hotel receptionist. Such creatures had to make do with the drovers' flop house, or a hay loft above the livery stable.

'This is most irregular, sir,' he blustered, trying not to outwardly display his revulsion that a squaw should be accorded a room in this most

205

prestigious establishment.

'And why is that?' enquired Kyte thrusting out his jaw. 'Do you have some specific objection to my lovely guest?'

'Well . . . erm . . . '

'Could it be that she is of a different origin to you, is that it?' persisted Kyte looking the wriggling worm squarely in the eye. He knew the score but was determined that prejudice of this nature should be addressed firmly. The girl had saved his partner's life and deserved better.

'I will have to consult the manager,' announced the clerk, hurriedly vacating the lobby.

'You do that,' snapped the colonel after his retreating back. 'In the meantime, she can have room number six.' He leaned over the counter and extracted the appropriate key from the line of hooks behind. Largo had been looking on with his arms crossed in a nonchalant stance. An amused smile creased his mouth. He followed Kyte who took hold of his guest's arm and guided her up the wide staircase to the upper floor of the hotel.

It was little more than ten minutes later that a tenuous knock came on the door.

'Enter!' Kyte deliberately injected a pompous tone into his summons.

A small rather corpulent man stuck his balding head round the door.

'The manager, I presume?' voiced Kyte peering down his angular nose.

Rubbing his hands uncomfortably, and bowing obsequiously, the official arrowed a timid look at Conchita. His button snout wrinkled.

'I regret, sir,' he began, 'that the hotel policy is that rooms should only be allocated to those persons of er . . . shall we say . . . an acceptable background. Such as yourself.' Here he cast a disdainful glance towards the smirking Largo. 'And possibly others of similar origin.'

'You say what yuh like,' butted in Largo. 'To my way of thinkin', Conchita bein' the daughter of a full-blooded Kiowa chief and medicine man is a far more acceptable background than some I could mention.' A pervasive glare skewered the sweating manager to the floor. Unclasping the knife Conchita had given him, Largo proceeded to clean his fingernails. The hint was subtle but clear.

Kyte said nothing. He merely studied the little man without speaking, relishing the toad's embarrassing discomfort.

Then he said, 'Would it make any difference to the hotel's policy if I were to offer double the going rate for the room? I will of course be wanting three rooms for a minimum of one week's stay. Possibly longer.' Kyte extracted a wad of greenbacks from inside his jacket. 'Payment in advance of course.'

On hearing this declaration, the sycophantic manager's beady eyes popped. His manner changed abruptly. Now all smiles, he slavered as the dollar bills floated before his ogling gaze.

'I am sure that on this occasion, the

hotel can accommodate your needs and wishes, Colonel Kyte,' he prattled.

'I never doubted it,' effused Kyte, hustling him unceremoniously out of the door. 'And now for some privacy if you will.'

The door slammed shut.

'Easy eh?' smirked Kyte.

'White-man's money open any door,' agreed Conchita. 'I am in your debt.'

'You helped the boy here out of a pickle he had gotten himself into.' A thumb hooked towards his partner. 'Least I could do to remedy matters.'

★ ★ ★

Next morning after breakfast, the two man-hunters made ready for an early start. Their intention was for Conchita to remain at Fort Sumner. When told of this, she adamantly refused to be left behind. No amount of persuasion concerning the danger involved could persuade her otherwise. The girl's mind was made up. After all she had suffered at the hands of Texas Jack Cantrell and his Red River Gang, Conchita wanted to be actively involved in the final denouement.

Didn't they owe her that chance?

Largo had to agree with her sentiments. Kyte shrugged resignedly as he mounted up and spurred off down the main street.

As they were passing the military stockade, Conchita called for them to rein up.

'I call here to see cousin,' she said. 'He army scout. Get something off him.'

'What might that be?' asked Largo.

The girl smiled, 'You see.' Then she nudged her horse through the main gate leaving the puzzled duo shaking their heads.

Fifteen minutes later, the girl appeared toting a longbow and quiver of arrows.

'You gunfighters,' she announced perkily, 'Conchita also now fully armed.' She could not fail to heed the two men shaking their heads in disbelief.

Meeting their cynical frowns, she

notched one of the arrows into the bow string and pointed to a clump of bushes some fifty yards away. After a minute a prairie chicken emerged pecking at the ground. The zing of the arrow being released was almost immediately followed by a choking squawk.

'Fresh meat for supper,' grinned Conchita, positioning the bow across her shoulders. Whooping and hallooing with glee, the girl kicked off to recover her trophy leaving the two men gaping open-mouthed in stunned awe.

Conchita was sure one helluva gal. And they both loved her for it.

It would take the best part of two full days to reach the ferry crossing at Bittersweet. Largo prayed they would not be too late. If Cantrell had already crossed to the far side, it would throw their plans into total disarray. But travelling from Buckeye, the gang had been forced to cross the Devil's Playground. That notorious stretch of soft sand would inevitably have slowed them up.

That was what he was counting on.

For much of the way, they followed the west bank of the Pecos downstream. Deviations were necessary where the river plunged through deep ravines. But for the most part, the river meandered across a wide arid plain. The only vegetation was a mixture of dwarf willow and stunted cottonwoods that clung tenaciously to the water's edge.

A blistering sun beat down in unrestrained fury and they all thanked nature's bounteous hand for the presence of this mighty river — a sure guide and life force amidst the barren desolation that encompassed the Chaves Plateau.

13

Bittersweet Crossing

Texas Jack was worried. The frown lines etched across his forehead stood proud like the ribs of a dead buffalo. Since the previous afternoon, the gang had been camped at Spider Rock awaiting the arrival of Cherokee George. They had sat around smoking and playing cards, Cantrell becoming increasingly agitated.

'He shoulda been here long ago,' opined the gang boss, his eyes hawkishly scanning their back trail. 'Somethin' bad's happened. I kin feel it.'

'Maybe he's gotten hisself lost,' suggested Mangas Pete haltingly.

Cantrell scoffed at the intimation. There was a bitter cut to his acerbic response. 'George is the best tracker in the territory. He'd never get lost. I reckoned on him gettin' here afore us by cuttin' through the mountains.' The skin tightened over Cantrell's taut features. 'No!' he stressed, pacing up and down. 'It's that damn bounty killer. Somehow he's gotten free and done fer George.'

'Thee *bastardo* must have had help,' said Mendoza.

'Yeh,' drawled the gang leader musing hard on this viewpoint. 'And I know who from.'

Conchita!

Now it all made sense. He'd noticed her eyeing him up. Nothing too obvious. Could she have known all along who he really was? Maybe it was the Kiowa in her. That witchdoctor father must have passed on the spiritual ability to read minds, see things as they were.

Cantrell snarled. He'd been taken in, well and truly hoodwinked. And by a blasted Indian squaw. Eyes flinty and black as coals, his balled fists raised in impotent fury. But they wouldn't get away with it. No way. Texas Jack Cantrell's mind was made up. Once they'd done the bank at Contention, he'd make it his business to hunt them both down. Only then would he split up the gang.

Now they were one man down, perhaps he could persuade Humpback Thomas at Bittersweet to join them. The old soak was well past his hell-raising days, but he'd be OK for holding the nags outside the bank.

'Strike camp,' he rapped tersely. 'We've wasted enough time already.'

Within fifteen minutes, the four riders were spurring their mounts across the loose scree below the surging thrust of Spider Rock.

★ ★ ★

Towards late afternoon of the second day, Largo called a halt as the tiny cluster of wooden shacks and lean-tos that comprised the Bittersweet Crossing hove into view. A sprinkling of the graceful desert yucca known as Our Lord's Candlestick surrounded the trading post. Interspersed with prickly pear in full bloom, they gave the place a deceptive allure, an inviting oasis amidst the aridity. And red chilli peppers hanging up to dry only served to enhance the illusion. For illusion it surely was.

Bittersweet was no *paraiso desértico*, merely a temporary haven for outlaws on the dodge. A place where, for a brief spell, they could rest awhile. For a price, Humpback Thomas, the proprietor, would supply them with victuals and entertainment courtesy of two Comanche squaws well past their bloom of youth. Nobody knew whether Thomas was his first or last name. The Quasimodo-like hunch had been his sole means of identification as far back as anyone could remember.

As well as the trading post, Thomas operated the ferry service to the far bank of the Pecos. Bittersweet was the only spot within fifty miles where the river narrowed sufficiently to enable it to be negotiated in safety. The ferry itself was little more than a bed of logs tied together with a plank decking. Linking by a two-inch cable stretched across the hundred yard gap, it was operated by a winch with pulleys fixed to stout supporting poles on each jetty.

From their vantage point on a rocky promontory overlooking the ferry cross-ing, the three hunters had a fine view of any riders approaching Bittersweet. Only one horse stood tethered outside the main log cabin. So at least they had arrived in time. That is unless Cantrell and his boys had already crossed and were now well on their way to Contention. The notion found a dark cast settling over Kyte's face.

Tight-lipped he voiced his concern to the others.

Another thought occurred to Con-chita.

'Maybe horses in barn.' She pointed to a wooden building over to the left. 'Cantrell could be here already.'

Largo nodded in agreement.

'Hadn't thought about that,' added

Kyte. He withdrew both his revolvers and checked the loadings, then announced, 'I'm going down there to take a look see. Keep me covered.'

Largo levered a shell into the breech of his Winchester.

'Take care,' whispered Conchita, laying a hand on the old gunfighter's arm. A coyote howled in the distance. Meadowlarks twittered vociferously to each other. Nature was going about its everyday business in the desert.

Kyte smiled.

'Don't you fret none about Sebastian Kyte,' he grinned. 'An old soldier like me knows a thing or two regarding stakeouts.'

Slipping down behind a cluster of rocks, he descended a gully and was soon lost to sight. They waited expectantly. Kyte would have to cross a stretch of open ground to reach the trading post.

Suddenly he appeared from behind a large boulder. Exposed to full view from the cabin, he bent low scuttling across the sandy clearing. The two watchers tensed, Largo's finger tight on the trigger of his carbine. Conchita could only watch. She was well out of range for the bow and arrow to be effective.

Halfway across the clearing, the cabin door opened and a man stepped out onto the veranda. In one hand, he held a glass, in the other a smoking cigar.

It was Rufe Claybourne.

Hidden by the dark shadow thrown by the sun's slanting rays, Kyte failed to notice the outlaw.

Not so Claybourne. Dropping the glass, he slapped leather, hauled out his pistol and cut loose. Caught by surprise, the outlaw's first shot went wide. A plume of sand leapt up some four feet right of his target. The second hit the mark, taking Kyte in the guts. Blood spurted from the telling shot. The old gunfighter staggered back a pace, desperately clawing at the weapon that ought to have been in his hand.

But he was too slow.

A third shot struck him high on the left shoulder, spinning him like a top. Throwing up his arms, Kyte slumped to the ground. Claybourne yelled in triumph. Stepping off the veranda, he advanced, gun at the ready to provide the terminating slug.

The shooting had taken the watchers by surprise.

Largo stiffened, his cheek resting against the rosewood stock of the Winchester. His finger tightened on the trigger. He had to be on target. There would be no second chance to save his partner from certain death.

But the lethal exchange had not gone unnoticed.

Inside the cabin, Cantrell jumped to his feet, upsetting the table and the meal he had been eating. Palming his revolver, he dashed over to the window and peered out. Mangas Pete slammed the door shut and moved to another opening at the far side.

'Who ees the *gringo* that Rufe shot?'

In his lyrical twang Dogface Mendoza was voicing what the others were thinking. Unable to obtain a clear view of the stricken bounty killer, none of them recognized Sebastian Kyte. Nor had they any idea that it was his daughter they had gunned down during the Alamagordo hit.

Suddenly, a deeper more resonant crack split the ether.

Claybourne staggered as a rifle shell took him in the right arm. The revolver flew out of his grasp.

'And he must have a sidekick backin' him up,' bellowed Mangas, smashing the glass with his pistol.

At that precise moment, Claybourne's head exploded like a ripe melon, blood and gore spewing from the fatal shot. The big man was dead before his shattered torso hit the ground.

'Did you see where that bushwhacker's holed up?' snapped Cantrell, a hint of panic lacing his words.

'Sure did,' replied Pete, excitedly

jabbing his pistol towards the rocky knoll at the far side of the clearing where Largo was secreted. The drifting whiff of smoke from the Winchester was a sure giveaway.

Immediately, a hail of bullets spat from three revolvers. But they were well out of range for handguns. A peal of laughter echoed back from the ambusher's perch. 'You'll have to do a heap better'n that, Cantrell.'

Largo followed up his taunting riposte with a more potent volley from the Winchester. Splinters of glass flew everywhere as a small pane shattered inwards.

Humpback Thomas screamed as a jagged sliver ripped his cheek.

Ignoring the proprietor's yelps, Cantrell emitted a vociferous stream of abuse finishing, 'It's that no-good bounty killer. I'd recognize that damn-blasted voice anywhere. If he figures on bestin' Texas Jack Cantrell, I'll see him in hell first.' But the gang leader knew that this was no time for futile outbursts of anger.

Action was needed.

'You got any rifles in this flea pit?' he spat, turning on the hunchback.

Thomas ignored the blunt query, continuing to whine as he dabbed a grimy bandanna against the bleeding cut.

Growling acidly, Cantrell swung his revolver towards the grumbling man. 'Cut out that gripin' and cough up some long guns,' he growled. 'That is if'n you don't wanna end up like old Rufe out there.'

The gang-leader's threat saw Humpy aiming a thumb towards a locked cupboard against the far wall. Cantrell grabbed the proffered key and hurried over to the stash. As he approached, the two squaws cowered back seeking to blend with the squalid surroundings. Cantrell's interest in them had dissolved after the first shots were fired.

Inside the cupboard were three Winchesters and a .50 Sharps buffalo rifle together with enough ammunition to hold off a small army.

A grunt of satisfaction hissed from between Cantrell's pursed lips. Grabbing hold of the Sharps, he moved back to his position by the window, making certain to punch out any loose shards of glass. The Sharps could pick off a jaybird at 600 yards. Poking it through the window, he lined up on the rocky outcrop from where the puff of smoke had risen. He waited until a movement caught his eye, then pulled the trigger.

The heavy rifle boomed loudly in the confined space of the cabin. A second later he yelled in delight as a hat flew into the air.

'Good shootin', boss,' cheered Mangas, pumping a couple of shots towards the distant bushwhacker. 'Think yuh got him?'

Largo had been careful to maintain a low profile since finding that the Red River Gang were ensconced within the trading post. But following the shooting of his partner, he had become overly concerned for his fate. Kyte was stuck in the open, slap bang in the line of fire.

Was he already dead? Largo peered down anxiously trying to pick up on any movement from the wounded man.

For a while he feared the worst.

Then he saw it. A slight shift of the right arm, followed by a leg. He was clearly in a bad way, and knew it. Ever so slowly, Kyte began crawling towards a clump of twisted thorn and juniper.

Carbine shouldered, Largo lifted himself above the level of the rock behind which he was concealed. His intention was to keep the gang occupied and thus prevent them from impeding Kyte's effort to seek cover.

The resounding boom from a heavy calibre long gun took him by surprise. It lifted his hat, and almost his hair. A burning tingle lanced his scalp as the bullet whistled by ricocheting off the rock wall behind.

'Cripes!' exclaimed Largo. 'They've got a Sharps in there.' The harsh crack was unmistakable to a rannie who knew his firearms.

Conchita pulled him down, both of

them huddling behind the rock palisade. Her gently probing fingers traced the dent across his head. They came away sticky with blood.

'You one lucky fella,' she sighed with relief. 'Only flesh wound.' Slithering down the back slope to where the horses were tethered, she said, 'You wait there. I get cure.'

Largo smiled briefly before drawling, 'I ain't goin' nowhere, sister.' His grey eyes crinkled as he gave a baffled shake of his tousled hair. 'You gotten a cure for everything in that there saddle-pack?'

'Me daughter of White Bear,' she stressed proudly.

The soothing balm stopped the bleeding and soon dispersed the thumping headache hammering at his skull.

Largo wasn't used to showing gratitude to anybody. He merely nodded. His normally hard features softened momentarily, then he retrieved his hat.

Poking a finger through the inch wide hole in the crown, he scowled. 'This

Stetson cost me ten bucks.' At least it kept the unremitting sun from burning a hole in his injured head.

Following the near miss, he made certain not to expose himself, keeping watch on the cabin from around the side of the rock.

For the next hour, both factions kept up a desultory fire.

Conchita cast an occasional eye towards this strange white man who had come into her life. He was different from the others. Her stoic demeanour relaxed slightly, as she realized her feelings towards Largo were not those expected from a Kiowa squaw. It was something that would have to be faced later. That is if they emerged from this tight spot in one piece.

Largo's attention was focused on the cabin and its hard-bitten occupants.

Sporadic and random, the gunfire merely served to remind the other side to keep on their toes. But with no easy targets, they were in what could only be termed a Mexican stand-off. Except that the outlaws held all the best cards. They had water, unlimited ammo and food. Not to mention shelter from the blistering heat.

Kyte would be suffering more than any of them. Largo couldn't helping perceiving that he had stopped moving, and only two yards from the juniper thicket. If he wasn't rescued soon, the sun would surely finish him off.

Something had to be done.

14

Showdown

Over to the left of the cabin, a stand of dwarf willow angled away from the river. The trees were out of sight of the cabin. Largo surmised that if he could cross the open ground without being seen and circle around behind the barn, he would stand a better chance of being able to surprise the gang from the rear. Conchita could maintain a steady rate of rifle fire to keep the gang's attention focused on the front.

After explaining his plan to the girl, Largo slid crab-like down a gully of loose stones behind his vantage point. Hidden from prying eyes, he was able to stand up and stretch his aching muscles. Squeezing between desiccated clumps of thorn, their spiny tentacles plucked at his shirt. Over to his left, a prairie dog disturbed from its lunch squealed before scuttling off into its burrow.

The descent to valley level was soon accomplished. Largo cast a wary eye towards the cabin. From this angle he was pleased to note that only the side was in view. The muffled crump of rifle fire told him that Conchita was playing her part in distracting the gang.

One final check that his position had not been imperilled and Largo was scooting across the open sward as fast as his high-heeled boots would permit.

Inside the cabin, Cantrell was feeling the pinch. He wanted to be away. Now this. They were pinned down and stuck in this miserable flea pit.

'I do not theenk there can be many of them,' intoned Mendoza from his post at one of the broken windows.

'How d'yuh figure that?' enquired Mangas.

'All thee shots, they come from same place.' Mendoza had more reason than either of the others for wanting Largo's head on a platter. It was a question of saving face, *machismo*. No Mexican could live with himself if he were to lose the respect of his *compañeros*. And Dogface had a lot to prove. His face creased in an ugly snarl.

'That's good thinkin', Dogface,' effused Cantrell nodding. 'Maybe there's only that sonofabitch Largo up in them rocks now that his sidekick has been sent packin'.' Cantrell massaged his chin in thought. They could hole up here indefinitely. But the bank at Contention had to be hit the following day, if his information about the dough being held in its vault was correct.

Then his black eyes lit up. He called Mangas Pete over to join him.

'You're the most agile of the three of us, Pete,' waxed Cantrell slapping his weaselly cohort on the back. 'Think yuh can sneak up behind that dude and stick him with that shiv of your'n?'

'Easy as takin' candy from a baby,' jeered the little guy, curling his lip in disdain. 'That dude won't know a thing about it.'

'We'll keep him occupied from this side,' added Cantrell as the weasel slipped out of the back door.

Having gained the tree cover without being seen, Largo bent low to pass behind the corral. A number of horses snickered at his approach, but his gentle soothing quickly calmed them down. Soon he was sidling along the back wall of the barn. Pausing at the corner, he checked the Colt Frontier was fully loaded then peered round the edge. Nobody there. So far so good. Ghost-like, he slipped over to the side of the cabin. This was the side unaffected by the action.

Thick log walls interspersed with tiny windows made it an impregnable fortress for even an army platoon to breach. Largo's face broke in a thin smile. Guile and a degree of wily cunning were needed.

The small window was still intact. With infinite care, he eased along the rough wall to peer through the glass.

Pete was about to cross to the barn when he saw Largo hugging the cabin wall no more than ten feet away. Momentarily he was stunned into immobility. How had the bastard managed to get this close without being spotted? It was of no consequence now. All that mattered was fixing him proper.

But not with a revolver. Drawing his pistol and cocking it would alert the guy. Pete's face cracked in a mirthless grin. His favourite weapon would do the job.

Soundlessly he withdrew the ten-inch bowie from inside its sheath and crept up behind his quarry. His potent gaze, icy and frozen, cemented onto Largo's back. The knife lifted ready for the killing strike.

Even though the window was caked in dirt, the sunlight gave it a mirror-like quality. That phenomenon is what saved Largo's bacon. The movement behind him was reflected in the glass.

Spinning in one fluid motion, he

triggered a shot at the lunging weasel. It took Mangas Pete in the neck. Severing the carotid artery, a stream of crimson spurted from the fatal wound. Pete staggered, arms waving frenetically. A look of stupefaction had replaced the arrogant sneer. His eyes blanked out, the lean face blanching as his life force rapidly ebbed away. A choking gurgle was his last utterance before he plunged forward, dead in a heap.

Blue smoke snaked skywards from Largo's .44.

But the bounty-hunter had not escaped unscathed. Indeed, he was seriously hurt. Mangas might be dead, but the momentum of his thrust had found its mark. The lethal knife protruded from the loose flesh on Largo's hip. Luckily for him, the steel blade had been deflected by his cartridge belt.

Tight-lipped, he dragged the dripping weapon clear, wincing as bolts of pain bit deep. Attempting to stem the flow of blood with his left hand, his one thought was to get away. Largo knew there was no time to lose. His cover was blown. All he could do now was hightail it and hope to try again later.

Dogface Mendoza had other ideas. Bursting through the rear door, he grinned evilly at his traitorous ally. Largo was bent over, his square jaw straining to suppress the throbbing pains that racked his body. As well as the gash in his side, blood dribbled from beneath his hat where the scalp wound had opened up. Not life-threatening in themselves, his injuries were nonetheless debilitating, energy sapping.

'Lying skunk!' howled Mendoza, his mashed proboscis briskly twitching, 'I trust you and take you as my *amigo*, only to find you are nothing but a *fetido* bounty killer. You make fool of Juan Castillo de Mendoza. Treat him like *payaso*. And nobody, least of all some back-shooting *gringo*, gets away with that.'

He was dancing around, hopping

from one foot to the other like a scalded cat. So smitten with rage was the ranting Mexican, so eager to avenge his bruised *machismo*, that he completely overlooked Conchita's presence over in the scattering of rocks and scrub vegetation at the other side of the clearing.

★   ★   ★

For the next ten minutes after Largo had made his play to break the stand-off, Conchita had maintained a regular rate of fire with the Winchester. Reloading the thirteen-round carbine for the third time as he had showed her, she suddenly found there were only five shells remaining in the cartridge box. They were soon used up.

What to do now? Cantrell was no fool. He would soon realize that his adversaries had run out of ammunition.

From this position high up on the rocky platform above the cabin, her bow and arrow were useless. But if she were to move down the slope taking advantage of the rock and vegetation cover available, she would be much closer to the cabin if the opportunity to assist Largo were offered.

Time was of the essence. Slinging the bow across her shoulders and the quiver crosswise, she made her way carefully down through the chaotic splay of boulders, ensuring at all times that she stayed out of sight. At ground level, she positioned herself in a gap between two boulders.

A groan caught her attention nearby. It was Sebastian Kyte. He was still alive.

Mendoza had finally come to the end of his vitriolic harangue. His breathing pumped out in short gasps. He had verbally at least assuaged his conscience. Now was the moment to physically terminate the object of his venomous invective. His finger tightened on the trigger. A lurid smile revealed smoke-yellowed teeth.

'Say your prayers, Banner, or whatever you call yourself,' he snarled.

The gun pointed. To Largo's befuddled brain it looked like a cannon.

At the moment of certain death, a saviour in the form of a quail-feathered arrow punched the Mexican back. The gun spewed forth its lethal cocktail of hot lead, but the bullet missed its target by a racoon's whisker. Largo felt the singeing heat as it whistled past his ear. Mendoza threw up his arms, his mouth flapping like a landed catfish. But no utterance emerged. Only a vain grappling with the air before surrendering to the grim reaper's embrace.

Overhead, a pair of buzzards circled. Their black profiles were etched starkly against the sky's azure back-drop. Desert predators smelt death from afar, and its aftermath was an unexpected feast.

Inside the trading post, Texas Jack was sweating. And not on account of the heat. Already the sun was making its routine passage towards the western horizon. The gang leader had intended to have crossed the Pecos by this time and be well on his way to Contention.

Now his plans for one last big job had been scuppered by this meddlesome bounty killer.

'What yuh gonna do then, Jack?' enquired an equally concerned Humpback Thomas. He had acquired his own bounty some years back for killing a bartender serving watered down liquor. Nobody had come looking for him at Bittersweet and he had forgotten about the incident. The arrival of Largo had brought the lurid memories flooding back in all their grizzly detail.

Cantrell was at the back door staring down at the corpse of what had been his best man. Now he was the only one left. But Largo was at his mercy. That is if'n he didn't show himself and let that Kiowa squaw get a bead on him. He had overlooked the fact that she was such a dab hand with the bow.

Keeping back from the line of sight, he palmed his hogleg. Largo was stunned. Now was his chance. An ugly grimace matched the icy glint in his eyes.

Suddenly, an arrow thudded into the woodwork of the door frame, quivering no more than a foot from his head.

'Kill Largo and I kill you.'

The cogent threat, blunt and chilling, echoed across the clearing. Bouncing off the surrounding cliffs, it slapped Texas Jack in the face. His gun hand wavered. He could just haul off and waste the varmint. But then he would be trapped. There was no way that he could escape the notice of a keen-eyed assassin.

Cantrell had witnessed the squaw's expertise with a bow and arrow on more than one occasion when they were out hunting fresh meat. Conchita had a lot of hate in her heart and Jack knew he had used her badly. It was too late for recriminations now. She would stay out there indefinitely. Indians were like that. Almost inhuman when roused. At one with the earth.

Perhaps he could wait her out.

'How much water we got?'

Thomas nodded towards the blackened coffee pot.

'Last dregs in there,' The cracked voice was thick like river-washed gravel. 'Don't matter none. It'll be dark in a couple of hours. Then I could sneak out there and grab us a bucket from the well.'

'Ugh!' Cantrell snorted derisively. 'Afore you know'd it, that squaw would have slit yer gizzard wide open and be cookin' yer innards for supper.' He peered out of the small window trying to pinpoint their elusive adversary. It was a fruitless expectation. 'You don't know Indians, Humpy. Only contact you've had is with them shagbags yonder.' He slanted an undisguised glower of contempt towards the two squaws who were still cringing in the corner.

Cantrell was only too well aware of how lethal a cocktail the Kiowa squaw could be. Squint Muldoon had paid a deadly price for underestimating her thirst for retribution when riled. Anticipating some after-dinner entertainment of a more earthy nature behind Santa

Fe's main thoroughfare, Muldoon had ended up being sliced open, his entrails dragging in the dirt. Only the sharp eye and quick-witted reactions of Mangas Pete had prevented the obdurate squaw from escaping the gang boss's clutches.

The realization that Cantrell had only escaped a similar fate by always having his gang in close attendance made his blood run cold.

Now that they had been wiped out, so too had his cool arrogance as he added, 'A true redskin can last for days in terrain that'd finish off any normal jigger.'

'You mean they call on the spirits of their ancestors?'

'Some'n like that,' was the hesitant reply.

An icy shiver launched itself down Humpy's crooked frame. His gaunt features took on an ashen pallor. Grabbing a jug of moonshine, he slumped in a chair and poured himself a hefty measure, knocking it back in a single gulp. It was the only drinkable liquid remaining in the trading post.

'So what we gonna do?' His voice had cracked, like his nerve. But at least the hard liquor stopped his hands from shaking. How could a single person, and a squaw woman at that, turn a man's legs to jelly like this one was doing?

Cantrell knew he had to try and make a deal.

'What yuh got in mind, Conchita?' he shouted.

There was a pause while the Indian girl marshalled her thoughts.

'Let him go free and I go with you back to Texas,' she called. 'I willingly be woman of Texas Jack Cantrell. As you white eyes say, no strings attached.'

'Why would you wanna do that fer me?'

'Give Largo chance for life.'

'You taken more than a passin' fancy to him?' There was a sneering inflection in his tone.

The silence spoke for itself.

Cantrell was seething inside. His guts churning.

Could it be a touch of the green-eyed monster nudging at his vitals? He pushed the notion aside. But deep down, there was no denying that he had feelings for this woman. A squaw maybe, nevertheless, she was different from all the others he had taken. And he had always resented the fact that his blundering attempts to win her over had never been reciprocated. Always the cold, arrogant disdain, their coupling had been a purely physical need on his part. That was the reason he had abused her, treated her so badly. Could he trust her now?

A hard gleam pierced his black gaze. He smiled thinly and without humour. It didn't matter. All he wanted now was to get across the river and disappear. Form another gang in due course, and resume his old ways. And if Conchita was his ticket out of here, so be it. If she didn't live up to her promise, he could always get rid of her, permanently.

'What is your answer, Jack Cantrell?'

'OK,' he shouted back. 'I agree. You

come with me . . . willingly . . . and the bounty-hunter goes free.'

The outlaw felt, or rather smelt, a presence at his shoulder.

'What about me, Jack?' whinged the hunchback. 'That man-hunter might decide to take me in along with the others when he cashes in the reward posters.'

An abhorrent snigger of revulsion emerged from Cantrell's tight mouth.

'Don't worry none, Humpy,' he jeered. 'I'll see you right.' Then he pulled the hovering ferryman out of Largo's hearing before whispering, 'Keep hold of this jasper until I'm over the river. Then kill him.'

Thomas gurgled, his nerve rapidly reasserting itself. Then he replied lasciviously, 'Seems to me that you oughta be more than just beholden to me fer helpin' you out.'

Cantrell sighed then reached into his saddle-bag extracting a wad of greenbacks which he stuffed down the ferryman's greasy shirt front.

'That suit yuh?' he mocked.

But Humpy's greedy peepers were already counting the hefty bundle.

'Now don't let this bastard outa your sight,' pressed Cantrell levelling the smarmy ferryman with a baleful glower. 'He's slippery as an eel. Savvy?'

'Don't you worry, Jack,' smirked Thomas, jamming his shooter into Largo's ear. 'One false move and he'll be stokin' the fires of hell.'

But Cantrell was worried. With his gang decimated, the last person he wanted to place any trust in was an old soak like Humpback Thomas. He threw a hank of rope across the room, 'Tie him up good and tight,' he rapped. 'Then we can be sure he won't try nothin'.'

He stepped out of the cabin as Conchita was emerging from her place of concealment, an arrow notched in case of any false move on Cantrell's part.

As she glided across the open clearing, Cantrell felt a tingling in his loins. He prayed to some far distant entity that this time she would truly be his woman.

'Let me see him,' she said flatly.

'Bring him out, Hump,' Cantrell called over his shoulder.

Largo was in a sorry state, his entire left side soaked in blood.

'I must see to his wound,' pressed Conchita, concern etched across her strained face. 'Only then will I go with you.'

Cantrell was none too pleased, but he gave a curt nod.

'Be quick about it,' he snapped, 'I wanna be across the river and well on the way to the Texas border before sundown.'

Removing her medicine bag, Conchita expertly set to work, her touch sending shivers down Largo's spine. He held her gaze, staring deep into those limpid pools, wanting to hold her, tell her how much he cared.

Only a rusty croak issued from the dry lips.

'No talkin',' hissed Cantrell.

Once she had finished her ministrations, Conchita stood up. Her noble heritage was displayed for all to see in the proud bearing. Still holding Largo with a look that spoke of her thwarted regard, she said in a soft voice, 'I ready now.'

'Get yer hoss and meet me by the ferry,' ordered Cantrell brusquely.

Ten minutes later, Texas Jack and Conchita were aboard the rickety structure. The winch system enabled the passengers to wind themselves across the river. It was heavy work and required the combined efforts of them both to haul the heavy and cumbersome craft across the rippling waters.

When they were halfway across, two shots rang out from the vicinity of the trading post. Cantrell scowled. That fool Thomas had done the business too quickly. But at least he was finally rid of that darned bounty killer. There was no chance of being pursued now that Largo was buzzard bait.

'What those shots?' Fear mixed with suspicion laced Conchita's startled outburst.

'I didn't hear nothin',' shot back Cantrell.

'You have Largo killed.'

'Why would I do that?' he countered. 'It musta been Humpback finishin' off that other dude.'

Conchita knew different. She lunged at him. Screaming and howling in maddened fury, she raked his face with her nails. It took all Cantrell's strength to keep the incensed squaw from tearing his eyes from their sockets. But even a crazed Indian was no match for a hard-bitten outlaw of Cantrell's impressive bulk. Drawing his pistol, he stepped back and struck her twice across the head.

15

A Watery Grave

Humpback Thomas had decided to get rid of his unwelcome guest at the earliest opportunity. To hell with waiting for Cantrell and that damn squaw to reach the far bank of the Pecos. Hauling out his old dragoon, the hunchback shuffled crab-like towards his victim, an ugly leer breaking across the pock-marked contours of his face.

'This is where you get yours, mister.'

A shot rang out. Thomas jerked as blood gushed from his mangled right shoulder. His mouth gaped wide in total surprise, his head twisting slowly on the scrawny neck. Another shot took him full in the chest. Rubbery legs collapsed as he sank to his knees.

'Shoulda . . . made sure you were . . . dead,' he gurgled. Then, glassy-eyed, he keeled over in the dust.

'That you should, hunchback.'

Sebastian Kyte was gasping for breath, his own life fast ebbing away. Leaning against the parapet of the well, he let the revolver slip from his grasp.

'You still with us, old man?' The shock at finding his partner still drawing his ration of air was reflected in Largo's stunned response.

Kyte could only manage a strangled grunt before sliding down the side of the well. His head fell forward across his chest. Slowly he pulled out a pocket knife and threw it across the intervening space separating them.

Largo soon cut himself free. Shaking some movement back into his numbed hands, he then hauled up the water bucket and soaked his bandanna with the cooling liquid. After dabbing his partner's forehead, he squeezed driblets of moisture between Kyte's parched lips.

'Not too much all at once,' he muttered, wiping the older man's blistered face, 'else you'll get the cramps.'

The older man's face contorted in a series of racking spasms. Retching up a gout of blood, his eyes took on a milky sheen. To Largo, his situation looked bleak. The guy was sinking fast. Summoning up that last vestige of strength from his shattered body had been the final straw. And all to save his partner.

Largo's eyes filled up, tears welling as he held the dying man in his arms.

'Don't worry, Seb,' he mumbled, his voice faltering with suppressed emotion. 'I'll get you to a sawbones. We'll soon have you fixed up.'

Kyte grabbed at his collar with surprising strength for one so weakened.

'No time for that,' he croaked. 'You know as well me that I'm a gonner.' He shook his head when Largo attempted to protest. 'Just promise me that you'll get Cantrell . . . ' His voice was beginning to slur, the breathing punched out in harsh bursts. 'And don't forget to see Rachel is taken care of.' Another pause. 'Now that Jane's gone, she'll be left on her own.' He peered up at his partner. 'You agree?'

Largo looked away, trying to conceal the anguish twisting his granite features. Not trusting his vocals, he merely offered a curt nod. Kyte returned the acknowledgement. He was satisfied.

'Now go get him . . . partner.'

Largo turned back to answer the wounded man. Blank eyes stared back at him. But there was no life there anymore. Sebastian Kyte was dead.

Gently laying the body down, he stood up whispering, 'Don't fret none. I'll be back to see you get a decent burial next to your daughter . . . old man.'

Pulling himself together with a jerk, Largo knew that time was of the essence. He grabbed one of Kyte's revolvers and stuck it into his belt, then dashed round to the jetty behind the trading post. The ferry was a little over halfway across the river. Once Cantrell reached the other side, he could somehow scuttle the ferry and so prevent any pursuit.

Narrowed eyes scanned the craft. There appeared to be a scuffle taking place. Above the steady prattle of the undulating current, he could just make out the distraught wrangle of irate voices. Conchita must have heard the shots and reached the obvious conclusion that she had been betrayed. One minute the pair were grappling together, the next only Cantrell was left standing.

Had he killed her?

There was no way of knowing from here on the west bank. Largo knew he had to somehow stop the ferry reaching the far shore. And that meant putting Cantrell out of action. But not with a handgun.

Then he remembered.

The Sharps.

Sprinting back to the cabin, he located the old but efficient buffalo gun and thumbed in a cartridge. Returning to the jetty, he knelt down and rested the long barrel against the upright beam supporting the ferry cable. Licking his thumb he primed the sight then drew back the hammer. One shot! That's all he would have. In the dimming light, the outlaw's silhouette stood proud against the pale horizon as it heaved on the cable winch.

The ear-cracking blast was followed almost immediately by a piercing cry.

Cantrell threw up his arms, clutching at his punctured torso. Shocked surprise etched his gaunt features. Even from that distance, Largo could see the red stain rapidly spreading across his front.

The outlaw cursed loudly, knowing it was a killing shot that had taken him. He could feel his life blood pumping out. This was the end of the line. Beaten by a tinhorn bounty killer and a squaw. A howl of rabid frustration issued from the open mouth.

But Cantrell was not finished yet. There was no way that he was going out with a whimper. Texas Jack would have the last laugh. Stumbling over to the tool box, he extracted a small hatchet and set to work on the taut cable.

Chop! Hack! Chop! Hack!

Two miles downstream were the Penasco Rapids after which the mighty Pecos plunged over a foaming cataract known as the Dragon's Pitch. That would be the end of the lovely Conchita and that bastard could do nothing to save her.

Largo fumed, his fists balling impotently. All he could do was look on helplessly as the stricken desperado went about this last wanton act of defiance.

Cantrell uttered a frenzied cackle. It was his final utterance. A splurge of crimson poured from the gaping maw.

As he breathed his last, the cable was almost severed. Only a few strands now held the ferry in place. Cantrell reeled drunkenly. The axe slipped through his nerveless fingers into the river. It was followed immediately by the dead outlaw.

The last Largo saw of him was an arm waving above the grey torrent beckoning his nemesis to follow. It was as if he was saying, 'Come on, you sonofabitch, follow me into the jaws of Hell.'

A sharp crack split the air as the last strands parted. Straight away, the ferry seemed to shiver as if knowing it had been released from its bondage. It yawed wildly, swinging round, and dragging the rest of the cable out of its supporting pulleys. Caught by the surging current in midstream, the flimsy craft was swept away.

There was no time for idle speculation. Largo gave a piercing whistle. On the far side of the bluff, Dancer's sensitive ears pricked up on hearing the summons. She was soon by his side. Mounting up, Largo followed the bucking ferry downstream as it began its perilous journey. He could make out the familiar tan buckskins of Conchita's still form. Was she already dead? He had no way of knowing but knew he had to try and reach her — for his own sake as well as hers.

He spurred the grey mare along the riverbank to keep ahead of the drifting ferry, praying that it would not smash against some hidden rocks and disintegrate.

All too soon, the river entered a constricted gorge. The turbulent waters known as the Penasco Rapids bubbled and hissed alarmingly in the confined space. Thrown from side to side, the ferry bucked and twisted, its decking soon buckling under the unaccustomed strain. The two frantic horses whinnied in panic, stamping their iron-shod hoofs.

Largo howled impotently. Even if Conchita wasn't drowned, she could end up being stamped to death.

A half-mile further down, the river opened up again. But from his vantage point on the bluff overlooking the rapids, Largo could see the deadly falls disappearing into an opaque void.

The Dragon's Pitch!

He would have to act soon. But what could he do?

Then he saw what might be his only chance. For sure, it would be the only one he would get.

A rocky overhang stuck out from the flat-topped bluff he was following. The ferry would pass directly beneath. It would be a drop of about twenty feet. If he got it wrong . . . the notion didn't bear thinking about.

Quickly dismounting, he positioned himself on the edge. From this angle the ferry looked exceedingly small and was bucking and prancing worse than a wild bronc.

His mouth felt dry, rougher than a badger's rump.

Suddenly it was there, right beneath him. Kicking off, he launched himself into space. For one fleeting second, he thought he had gone too late. Then he hit the decking hard, rolling under the stomping hoofs. One caught him a hefty clout on the left shoulder. But he hardly felt it. His first priority was for Conchita.

Checking for a pulse, his initial

thought was that she was dead. There was nothing. And her lips were turning blue. Panic gripped him. Roughly he shook her, slapping her beautiful face. The girl was drenched, her skin cold and waxy.

'Wake up! Wake up!' he yelled, above the howling torment of the river. 'Yuh can't peg out on me now.'

The harsh treatment did the trick. A low groan cut through his own invective. Her eyes flickered.

'Thank the Lord,' Largo sighed with relief.

By this time, the ferry had been ejected from the gorge into a less turbulent and much broader reach. But the falls were less than one hundred yards away, and closing rapidly. The sun had disappeared behind the serrated rim of the high cliffs that reared up on the western side of the canyon. Orange and red streaks were fading to purple.

Unceremoniously, Largo lifted the girl on to the blue roan and climbed up behind. He kicked hard, urging the cayuse to jump into the river's whirling ferment.

'Come on, feller,' he encouraged, 'You can do it.'

But the horse was too frightened and refused to budge. The bobbing head jerked frantically as it neighed in terror. Again Largo dug his spurs into the horse's side, this time drawing blood. Still it wouldn't shift.

Largo scowled. A determined tightness clenched at his jaw.

There was only one thing left.

Drawing the revolver from his belt, he held it next to the bay's head and pulled the trigger. A thunderous explosion bounced off the canyon walls. But it did the trick. Rising up on its hind legs, the horse plunged into the raging waters. Largo pointed it towards the west bank where Dancer was waiting patiently. The second mount would have to take its chances.

Away from the middle section, the river's undertow was less severe and the roan was soon pulling hard towards the sandy shoreline.

Safe on the shingle inlet away from the grasping clutches of the Pecos, Largo cast his gaze towards the ferry that was at that very moment plunging over the darkening void of the Dragon's Pitch. He shivered inwardly at what might have been, then set about gathering brushwood for a fire. They were both chilled to the bone and wet through. Largo wrapped a saddle blanket around the girl's trembling body.

With warmth seeping into her perished frame, Conchita quickly began to recover from her ordeal. A cup of fresh coffee and a plate of beans could work wonders for dented morale, especially in the company of the man who had saved her life.

Largo drew hard on a cigar butt. Smoke twined away in the darkness. His grey eyes held those of the girl as he sat cross-legged enveloped by his own blanket.

'What you thinking?' she murmured.

Her words purred in his ear like melted chocolate.

'I reckon things ain't turned out so bad after all,' he mused, staring into the hypnotic allure of the dancing flames. 'There's bounty money lying about that needs collectin'. And with a sizeable pot sittin' in the bank at El Paso, the future is lookin' bright and rosy. I oughta be able to retire from this game and settle down. Maybe buy a spread and raise a herd of them new Herefords.'

Conchita leaned forward. Her dark eyes probed deep into Largo's inner soul.

'And what of me, Largo?' she murmured. 'Where does Conchita fit into these plans of yours?'

A wry smile broke across the stubbled contours, a playful teasing reflected in the grey orbs.

'Ain't quite figured that one out yet.'

Conchita sighed, then lay back against the saddle, her eyes closed.

A new start was beckoning.

We do hope that you have enjoyed reading this large print book.

Did you know that all of our titles are available for purchase?

We publish a wide range of high quality large print books including:
Romances, Mysteries, Classics
General Fiction
Non Fiction and Westerns

Special interest titles available in large print are:
The Little Oxford Dictionary
Music Book, Song Book
Hymn Book, Service Book

Also available from us courtesy of Oxford University Press:
Young Readers' Dictionary
(large print edition)
Young Readers' Thesaurus
(large print edition)

For further information or a free brochure, please contact us at:
Ulverscroft Large Print Books Ltd.,
The Green, Bradgate Road, Anstey,
Leicester, LE7 7FU, England.
Tel: (00 44) **0116 236 4325**
Fax: (00 44) **0116 234 0205**

Other titles in the
Linford Western Library:

PONDERFOOT'S DOLLARS

Ben Coady

Already under the threat of losing his farm and being shunned by the community, Jack Barley faces his biggest problem yet. The notorious Bannion brothers arrive to rob the local bank, tracked by a deadly US Marshal. To avoid danger, they hit on a scheme involving Jack: in return for his wife and son's safety, he must rob the bank ... Jack complies with their demands, but the marshal is suspicious and the money is missing — can he save his family?

THE BONANZA TRAIL

John Dyson

Dawson City was a rumbustious boom-town where whisky and champagne flowed. Men lost fortunes on the throw of a dice as thousands of greenhorns flocked into the Yukon's golden triangle. Hunter and guide Scope Mitchell was better equipped than most to survive the perils of the wilderness, but he had a battle on his hands when Frenchie Pete and his gang of thugs began stalking him. Would his lone rifle be a match for the outlaws?